GREEN FIRES BURNING

THE WORLD IS ABOUT TO CHANGE

EEMIANS

PAUL MCGOWAN

Green Fires Burning

The World is About to Change
by Paul McGowan

First printing edition 2024
Viceroy Press LLC
4865 Sterling Drive
Boulder, Colorado 80301
www.eemians.com

BOOKS IN THE EEMIAN SERIES

Book One

The Aurora Project

We were not the first

Book Two

Green Fires Burning

The World is About to Change

Book Three

The Secret of Eschaton

Endgame

Book Four

They Came First

In the Beginning

1

North of Athens, Greece, Twenty Years Ago

Midnight rain lashed the town with an unrelenting fury, the cobblestone streets swiftly becoming rivers under the weight of the torrential downpour. The droplets pounded so violently against the *psistaria*'s windows and rooftops, that neither Hector nor Nikolaos heard the door open that night.

The dark form rounded the corner and Hector reached for his weapon, but he wasn't quick enough. The intruder set one massive hand upon Hector's shoulder and the other on his head. With a twist and a snap, Hector crumpled to the floor.

"Who are—"

"I am Symmachus, and you will kneel before me," said the voice, and Nikolaos's knees hit the wooden floor, unbidden. "Do you tremble at the feet of God? Do you know who you are?"

Nikolaos dared to look up at the man towering over him. Though he could make out no details, the light from the table's flickering candles illuminated blue eyes that seemed to pierce through his soul. He lowered his eyes.

"Long ago, Fallen Angels took for themselves the daughters of Men, who bore them children, giants all—mighty men of old, men of renown. I have been watching you. You are one of us. You are one of the forgotten sons of God. The Sons of Nephilim."

"I-I-I—" stuttered Nikolaos. "This is blasphemy. You cannot believe—"

"Silence! Though you are yet weak, the Holy Spirit will descend upon you, and you will be made powerful. I will be your guide. You will take your place by my side; you shall act as my right hand. For there is much to do. We must prepare for the day the Lord Himself will come down from Heaven, crying out with the voices of the archangels and the trumpet of God, and the multitudes who sleep in the dust of the Earth will awake. Some to everlasting life, others to shame and eternal contempt.

We who have prepared the way will be caught up with those in the clouds to meet the Lord in the air. And so, we few Chosen will be with the Lord forever."

Nikolaos spread his palms flat on the floor. He dared not turn his head, though he was aware of Hector's lifeless body in a heap beside him. He did not want to see whatever horror remained in his dead friend's eyes.

Because something within him stirred at Symmachus's words. Something almost like longing.

As if reading these thoughts, Symmachus uttered a single mirthless *ha.* "Have you never wondered about your power? Have you never wondered why weak men turn to you for guidance? Why, when you speak, others listen?"

Symmachus lashed out with one foot, landing a forceful kick to the side of dead Hector's head. "Men such as these? Too pathetic to grasp and take what they truly want? Too willing to follow the will of others?"

Nikolaos stared at Symmachus's feet, unable to speak.

"Our ancient race will inherit the Earth and ensure our God's work is done. For it is we who must stop Man's unholy quest to build a paradise on Earth—there is but one Paradise—the paradise of Heaven. God wills us to do His bidding and answer the call to fight the ultimate battle."

Symmachus reached out a hand. "If you will take up your birthright, rise. You will be reborn as Uzziel, the strength of God, and you will sit at my table as a brother."

The longing within Nikolaos grew, expanding until it muffled any concerns he might have felt. He reached for Symmachus's hand. The man's skin was unnaturally cold, his grip unnaturally firm, and he pulled Nikolaos to his feet without effort.

"I will take up my birthright," said Uzziel, and when he followed Symmachus through the old *psistaria,* past the bodies of the men who'd been Nikolaos's friends, he did not look back.

~

Undisclosed Location, Present Day

UZZIEL prepared for his meeting with Symmachus with the utmost care. His master, he had learned over the years, valued precision in all things. Uzziel wanted nothing to distract from the good tidings he brought—the destruction of the Eemian pyramid in Antarctica, and the deaths of those who had thought to use its power against them.

Satsky was dead. Sawyer, dead. And though he had not seen every corpse, no one could have survived the Antarctic storms that had swept in as if guided by the very hand of God to smite their enemies.

Pleasure curled in his belly, warm and sinful; he had done all he set out to do. He alone had brought their enemies to their knees. He alone deserved praise for all he'd done. Symmachus would surely reward him above all others.

As swiftly as it had warmed him, that pleasure turned cold and sour.

Pride goeth before the Fall. The words echoed inside Uzziel's head as if Symmachus himself were in the room to whisper them.

If his driver were not already on the way, Uzziel would have immediately reached for his scourge. On one end of the weapon—the tool—a wooden handle, worn smooth as silk after years of fervent use. On the other dangled silvered chains, and the sharpened blades along their length sparkled in the shaft of light coming through the window.

Tonight, he would slash his own skin; the knives would cling to the sticky blood of his back. Through mortification of the flesh, he would be made clean and his pride would be forgiven.

As his phone buzzed to signal the arrival of his driver, Uzziel lowered a heavy gold cross around his neck. The weight was a reminder to focus on the holy purpose Symmachus had given him. A single life meant nothing. A single battle won did not mean he could turn away from the importance of the war.

Uzziel was nothing. Later, the scourge would sing that hymn against his spine, driven by the bassline beat of blood hitting the stones beneath his penitent knees.

The driver said nothing when he opened the door for Uzziel. He said nothing as he returned to his seat and drove to the sacred chambers. Although silence was not unusual, Uzziel's skin crawled. He did not recognize this man. He did not recognize this silence. And with pride still poisoning him, he feared everything that silence might portend.

When they arrived, the driver did not meet Uzziel's eyes.

Unsettled, Uzziel entered the compound through an archway overgrown with vines that still clung to the masonry, even in death. Above him, a cavernous stone ceiling soared into the darkness of the anteroom. His footsteps echoed in the ancient room. At the end of the long hall, a wooden door stained with deep black streaks filled the stone entryway. Uzziel pushed it open, and it groaned in protest.

The near-perfect blackness of the room beyond was broken only by light from the entrance behind him and cracks in the covered windows. Above him, ornate but rusting iron held what little he could see of the ceiling aloft. The room smelled of damp earth and decayed leaves.

In front of him, rows of pews led to the altar of this forgotten church. As his eyes adjusted to the dark, Uzziel made out the deeper darkness of the small alcoves set into the walls below the covered windows—alcoves where council members once knelt in prayer. Though he could not see its details in the shadows, he knew that the wall at the end of the nave was painted with an image depicting two hands reaching down from angry clouds above, reaching for the anguished souls rising from the Earth.

Uzziel knelt before the empty altar and lowered his head in silent prayer.

And he waited.

His knees began to tingle. To throb. But he was accustomed to such pain, and he turned his thoughts to his master—and to their God. Boots scraped against the stone floor as he kneeled alone in the chamber.

"Uzziel." Symmachus's deep voice reverberated through the cavernous hall.

Uzziel immediately stretched out his arms and lowered his upper body to the frigid stones that leeched the warmth from his flesh as if in holy exchange. His trembling fingers grazed the floor's crevices.

It was not enough.

"I have returned, Master," Uzziel said. And though he sought to remain neutral, in his voice, he heard the poison of his pride oozing between the syllables, demanding praise, demanding reward. "Those who stood against us have fallen."

Silence curled around his throat like a hand, and when that hand squeezed, Uzziel knew he had misjudged.

"Fallen," Symmachus echoed. "Fallen? Those who stand against us walk free, and the secrets I commanded you to gather are but motes of ash and dust buried under the ice."

"Your Holiness, I did not wish to see the Eemian secrets fall into the hands of our enemies. This is why I—"

"Silence! Your excuses only magnify your failure. The secrets you wished to protect are now in the hands of our enemies, the Quondans."

Uzziel was not foolish enough to speak, but he longed to plead for clemency, forgiveness. He longed to defend his decisions. His lips parted, but the memory of how swiftly Symmachus could end a life kept him silent lest his be the neck broken, the eyes left empty and staring.

"There are other secrets," Symmachus said. "Other sanctuaries."

"Then I will discover them, Master. I will—"

This time, a very real hand closed around Uzziel's throat. Squeezed.

"No, Uzziel. You have new orders. And if you fail to follow them, if you deviate from them by even a degree, your nightmares will seem a haven compared to what awaits you."

A cold sweat formed on Uzziel's brow, his neck. Droplets stung as they ran down the channel of his spine, taking the path his scourge would soon follow.

Symmachus brought his cowled head close to Uzziel's ear and whispered, "Fail me again, Uzziel, and no God will offer refuge from my wrath."

The words hung in the air long after Symmachus retreated like a wraith sinking into the underworld. Though Uzziel was alone, the weight of his task—and the chilling finality of Symmachus's warning—lingered, suffocating him with nearly the force of the hand that had closed around his throat moments before.

2

Private hanger, Ixtapa-Zihuatanejo Airport, Mexico, April 22

Dr. Harriet Bickford certainly knew how to command an audience.

The beer had been cold when she started her tale; by the time she finished, bottles had either been drained many times over or forgotten long enough to turn warm, condensation slicking the longnecks and causing labels to bubble.

"That's . . . a hell of a yarn, Doc," said John Grimes, twirling a dented beer cap between his fingers.

Her grin was small but impish. "Is it really so hard to believe now, after everything?"

The inclination toward skepticism was, of course, strong. The tale was outlandish, deserving of skepticism; it was the type of thing you'd find in a sensationalist documentary online, at the bottom of a deep, dark rabbit hole: *Technologically Advanced Cultures Inhabited Earth 100,000 Years Ago.*

Sam ran a hand along Sky's side, back and forth. "Just so I'm clear," he said, "you're saying that Eemians still exist?"

"You were there, Sam. You walked the halls. You saw their work, their art, with your own eyes." She gestured at the photos they'd printed from Sam's digital images. "Is there any doubt they ensured some manner of survival?" She paused. "Not for all, of course. It's impossible to save everyone. But for some number of them—can you really doubt it?"

Sam drained his bottle and reached for another, snagging a few extra cubes of ice from the cooler and dropping them between Sky's paws. The dog crunched happily on the frozen gift. "I don't doubt what I saw. I can't doubt it."

The wind picked up suddenly, swirling through the open aircraft hangar, threatening to scatter the photos. John Grimes collected the pictures, fanned out like a deck of cards, and tucked them safely under a laptop. He cleared his throat. "With all due respect, doc, the survival of their tech doesn't mean the people themselves are still walking around."

"How soon we forget," said Harry.

"Forget?" Grimes echoed.

"So you *haven't* forgotten about the graphene tablet Karl and I discovered in Chile some ten years ago?"

Grimes blinked once. Twice. "That particular yarn might've slipped my mind, yeah."

"You've been busy, so I'll forgive the lapse."

Under the table, Sky's ice was now a memory; the dog stretched and let out a long, loud groan before relaxing with a sigh. Everyone around the table exchanged an amused glance.

"Karl and I argued about it, you know. Constantly." Fondness warred with sadness, and Harry's smile pinched at the corners. "I'd always suspected the existence of ancient, technologically advanced civilizations, wiped out by some extinction-level event. But I never had any real proof."

Julia leaned forward, resting her elbows on the table and propping her chin in her hands. "And then you got your hands on that tablet and the piece of graphene, and things started looking possible." Her eyes narrowed. "Bet it still wasn't enough to convince Satsky."

"It most certainly was not." Harry chuckled. "And, objectively speaking, the evidence we *did* have wasn't compelling enough, never mind comprehensive enough, to make any claims about it."

"Biggest story in the world, and you had to keep it under your hat," Grimes said.

"Precisely, young man."

Grimes cocked an eyebrow, which gave Sam a very good idea of how long it had been since anyone had used those words to refer to him.

"We had a thoroughly modern material from the ancient past. You'd think that would have been enough, but whenever we mentioned it to our colleagues in the field, they received the news with heavy skepticism." She shrugged. "And for good reason, I suppose."

"They were still wrong," Julia replied.

Harry took a long sip from her bottle. "Science is a harsh mistress. She demands facts and evidence and proven hypotheses. And that isn't a bad thing." She ran a thumb across the glass lip, collecting a bead of beer. "Besides, you all have something none of them had."

After a few seconds of puzzled silence ticked by, Sam exhaled a short laugh.

Harry popped the cap of another longneck. "You know the answer already, Dr. Sawyer?"

Sam nodded. "Experience."

"Exactly so. Now, doubt is important. Without doubt, few of us would be propelled to discover adequate evidence of proof."

"Are you saying you found that proof?" Julia asked.

"I'll let you decide that for yourselves. A few years ago, I was in Vienna for a conference. A day or two after my talk, I decided to take a side-trip to Salzburg. Get in some sightseeing. While I was waiting for my train, a man approached me. A Dr. Lucas Milton—"

Julia's brow furrowed. "I've never heard of him."

Harry shrugged one shoulder. "Neither has anyone else. And yet, there he was. He claimed to have seen my talk. After a few minutes, the conversation changed." She paused. "Abruptly."

"How so?" Sam asked.

"Out of the damn blue, this complete stranger revealed that he knew about the graphene tablet we'd found in Chile, its purpose, and its origins."

Sam shook his head. "But there's no way—"

"Tell me about it. He even insisted he could provide clues about something he referred to only as the Light."

Harry paused again, but no one around the table interjected, Sam included. If storytelling wasn't Dr. Bickford's favorite part of teaching, it had to be high on her list.

"Now, before you all think I'm some kind of halfwit, I didn't want to admit I had the dang thing. It's not easy to break tenure, but smuggling an undeclared foreign artifact into the country might be just the thing to manage it. This Dr. Milton, whoever he was, was sympathetic to my position."

Grimes cleared his throat. "Begging your pardon, ma'am, but how in the hell did you come around to trusting this man?"

"He had information," she replied frankly. "Information that lined up with what I know—and some of what I suspected. He was the one who told me about the legend of the Eemians. He claimed he read the original text."

Here, Harry's skepticism showed in the tilt of her mouth, the narrowing of her eyes. But, like a passing storm cloud, it didn't last.

"That text—he claimed—described this thing he called the Light, telling of its potential and its dangers. When I asked to see the source material, as it were, he got very shy. A little squirrelly, if I'm honest. He claimed that these relics are handed down from trustee to trustee over generations. Been that way for the last five *thousand* generations, in fact."

"But no document could survive for that long," Julia interrupted, shaking her head.

"You sure about that?" Sam asked. "Because I'm thinking if it were inscribed on graphene, it'd have a hell of a shelf life."

Harry clapped her hands, like a teacher delighted by her star pupils. "There you have it. An entire culture's history and secrets, inscribed on dang-near-indestructible tablets."

"So that's what you and Satsky found in Chile," Julia said. "A piece of a history book, basically."

"Exactly, child. My train showed up and he vacated the conversation." Harry chuckled. "Something straight out of *The DaVinci Code,* I swear. Never saw him again."

"Is that where you heard about that little fairy tale you were telling us about earlier?" asked Grimes.

Slowly, Harry pulled her gaze from Grimes. The room went suddenly quiet. Her eyes seemed to search for something in the distance of the hanger.

"I am sorry, ma'am," stumbled Grimes "I..."

Without pulling her eyes from Harry, Julia put her hand up for quiet.

Harry set down her beer and, with her index finger, slowly traced the condensation down the bottle's side. "*Once upon a nightmare the end of the world came...*" she whispered.

Julia placed her hand on Harry's. "Where did you hear that? The stranger?"

Harry nodded, her eyes never leaving the frosty squiggles of condensation on the bottle.

"The light...the end of their world. It was a light that should have been their salvation, but instead..."

"Go on," said Sam, softly.

"We are pretty certain their references to *the light* are directly related to what Sam saw inside the pyramid and captured in these photos."

Harry pulled from the pile of photographs the picture of the huge machine Sam and Satsky had discovered. She pointed at the large silver donut-like shape in the center.

"Ever heard of a Stellarator?"

The group nodded *no* in unison.

"A Torus? Nuclear fusion?"

"As far as I know ma'am, a Torus is what the Mexicans call a bull and, as for this nuclear business, I 'spose you mean like Chernobyl? Fukushima? Three Mile Island kind of nuclear fusion?" asked Grimes.

"No, no, John. That's fission: nuclear power plants; nuclear waste; meltdowns. Fission produces energy by splitting apart atoms. Fusion is the opposite. Instead of splitting them apart we fuse them together to get energy out."

"Like how the sun works?" asked Julia.

"Exactly," said Harry. "Unlike fission, fusion is perfectly safe, produces no radiation, uses as its fuel the most abundant element in the universe, hydrogen, and its only waste material is water."

"What's that got to do with the Eemians?" asked Sam.

"We believe fusion—what they refer to as *The Light*—must have been their secret weapon against the impending climate disaster. It was to be their savior.

"Is that what this Dr. Milton fellow told you?" asked Grimes.

"No," sighed Harry, "not directly. Up until Sam's photographs inside the Eemian sanctuary, we had no clue what this light generator he spoke of was. Now, it's pretty clear."

Harry circled with her finger the large silver donut in the center of the photograph. "That huge machine you photographed inside their pyramid? It was a fusion power generator. Had to be. What we might today call a Stellarator."

"...and?" asked Sam.

"And that's the question we are asking ourselves. If they had the technology—and clearly, they did—why didn't it save them?" Harry shook her head. "Fusion is the key to our own civilization's survival. Our only means of breaking forever free the shackles of the carbon cycle. Unlimited energy to power our modern society without any downsides."

Julia reached over the table and picked up the Tootsie Roll-like Eemian artifact Sam had found inside the pyramid. She twisted it around in her fingers as one might marvel at a precious stone.

"Is that why you got so excited about this?"

"Exactly. We now know what it is and how it was used."

Julia handed the object to Sam.

"What you and Karl found inside that Eemian sanctuary," said Harry, "is one of two missing keys we need to unlock the secret of fusion that could insure the future survival of our planet. You found a substance we only dream about. Metalized hydrogen, the ultimate fuel for a fusion reactor. The Eemians had it. They had it all."

"If what you are saying is true," said Julia, "then why didn't it save them?

Harry slowly moved her head from side to side. "We know their civilization was wiped out by a climate crisis, one that appears to be mirroring our own. And, after Sam's discovery, we are pretty certain they had the technology to save themselves and, yet..."

"Go on," said Julia.

"Something unexplained happened. The scientist side of me wants to believe in the simple answers: too little too late, miscalculations, politics. The darker side of me is worried. "*Once upon a nightmare the end of the world came...*" she said softly.

"Here's the simple truth of it," said Harry, suddenly animated. "If we had fusion technology today, we could save our own planet from following a similar path to that of our Eemian ancestors."

"I'm sorry," said Grimes, "but I am still a bit lost. How is it that a professor of weather, or whatever it is you teach, Doc, knows so much about this fusion stuff?"

Harry laughed and popped the top off another bottle. "Not to sound stuffy, John Grimes, but I don't study the weather. I study the climate. Big difference."

"Yes, ma'am. Now, about that fusion business."

Harry smiled. "Like Julia said, fusion is what powers our sun and all the stars in the universe. For years now, we have been trying to figure out how to harness this power and generate electricity. It's a huge challenge. Like trying to bottle a miniature sun and then tapping into its energy. If we can do that, we have a chance at freeing our world from climate collapse."

"We?" asked Julia.

"Oh dear," said Harry, "I do suppose this is a lot to take in after all you three have been through."

"Ma'am?"

"I have much to tell you, and some of it...oh hell, *all of it* is going to sound a bit crazy. "We've made arrangements for you three to relax tonight, get your bearings, and then let's meet in the morning when our crew takes us back to Dallas."

Sky stood up and trotted towards the hanger door at the sound of car doors opening.

"Get some rest," said Harry, "tomorrow's conversation is going to be...well, life changing."

3

For Sam, Mexico was like a Jimmy Buffett song brought to life.

But only if that Jimmy Buffet song involved several near-death experiences—including, but not limited to, zealous madmen, killer robots, deadly explosions, and an Antarctic superstorm—before anyone poured the margaritas.

Even though Sam had already soaked up a full day's worth of sun and *cerveza,* his hands still ached with the memory of cold. He struggled to wrap his brain around the avalanche of new discoveries they'd made ... and the dozens of new questions those same discoveries swiftly spawned.

"Can't sleep?"

Sam turned and smiled as Julia approached. She was wrapped in one of the hotel's plush white robes, her feet bare and her hair damp from either a swim or another hot shower. He suspected the latter. With a rueful shake of his head, he waved at the lounger next to his. "I turned off the air conditioning and it's still too cold in there."

Julia ignored the other lounger and sat next to him on his, instead. "I'd tell you it's all in your head, but I just boiled myself in a hot bath because I can't shake the chill."

"Are we sure this isn't some bizarre *folie a deux?*"

Julia barked a laugh. "You mean, we're actually freezing to death somewhere in Antarctica right now, and this is our shared hallucination? I don't know. I think I'd dream up better water pressure."

"And better beer?"

"Definitely better beer."

"Tequila's been good, though." Possibly just a little *too* good. Sam's healthy appreciation for Patron Silver was swiftly on its way to becoming a full-blown love affair.

Julia grinned. "The tequila's what keeps people coming back. We can call it the Patron Tourism Initiative."

A short laugh escaped him. "Right. What nobody tells you is that the tequila keeps you coming back because you can't remember what happened the last time you visited. Solid strategy."

Julia's smile shifted into something sadder. "To be honest, I wouldn't mind forgetting the past few weeks." She shook her head. "Some stretches I could really do without."

Before he could think better of the decision, Sam reached out and placed a hand over one of Julia's. "Same here. But ... " He ducked his head. "I definitely wouldn't change making the acquaintance of one Dr. Julia Bassi."

"Ahh, is this the famed Texan charm I keep hearing about?"

"Could be," he said, slightly emphasizing his drawl.

Her grin widened. "You usually hide that little quirk, Dr. Sawyer. I was starting to think you weren't a real Texan at all."

Sam's hand still rested on top of Julia's. After a heartbeat of silence, she turned hers so their palms rested against each other.

"Maybe life's too short to keep hiding parts of me from everyone else." He paused. "Like an accent I've been trying to lose since undergrad."

She lifted an eyebrow. "Well, as long as you don't go full 'little lady' stereotype, I think it can stay."

"I'm telling Grimes you said that."

She made a face. "Someone should." As quickly as amusement lit her eyes, a shadow fell again. "I-I'm sorry about your friends, Sam."

"And I'm sorry about Satsky."

"They deserved better." She tilted her chin to look up at the sky, and he caught the glitter of tears on her eyelashes. "I hate that we had to leave them there. Just ... I hate it."

Sam squeezed Julia's hand. For the first time since Antarctica, his fingers almost felt warm. When she squeezed back, he shifted a little closer, until he imagined he could feel the heat of her along the side of his body even though they weren't quite touching.

With her gaze still fixed on the sky, she added softly, "I don't hate that we're here, though. Right now. Alive. Not frozen in a tent, buried alive."

Screw Patron Silver—the cocktail of grief and terror and relief was the headiest of them all.

"Survival's a funny thing," he said quietly. "We're programmed to pursue it. Deep down in the nuts and bolts of our DNA, we're hard-wired to fight for survival."

"But?" Julia prompted, shifting closer, near enough that her thigh brushed his and their arms touched.

Sam tried not to think about how warm her hand felt in his, or the fact that she was close enough for him to catch the scent of her shampoo on the breeze. "But when you survive and someone else doesn't ... "

She made a soft sound of agreement. "You wonder why you survived at all. Intellectually, you know it's a series of objective circumstances with no deeper meaning attached to any of it. And yet, sometimes objectivity isn't as satisfying as we'd like. It's still tempting to ask why."

"Asking why is what we do," he said. "Occupational hazard."

The sliver of moon barely reflected in the pool below.

Julia sighed. "If only someone could have explained that to my parents. Maybe my inability to stop asking wouldn't have driven them quite so crazy."

Sam bumped her shoulder with his but offered no similar anecdote. He'd have had to see his parents more often for them to get irritated with his endless questions. Luckily, he'd had books. The internet. Mrs. Sanchez, the long-suffering school librarian. Grimes, sometimes.

"Sam?"

He raised his eyebrows in a silent question. In answer, Julia rose to her feet, tightening her grip on his hand so he'd join her. She took a step backward, her eyes never leaving his. He followed. When they reached the terrace outside her room, he half-expected her to pull away, but she didn't.

He didn't ask why.

Occupational hazard aside, he was pretty sure he knew the answer, deep down in those nuts and bolts of his DNA.

Because we're here. Because we can. Because we survived what should have killed us at least two or three times over.

Because wrapped in each other's arms, they were finally warm.

4

Enroute to Dallas, Texas

The private jet was a luxury neither Sam nor Julia ever expected. From nearly freezing to death in Antarctica to traveling like the rich and famous, the four of them—Sky, Sam, Julia, and Grimes—felt completely out of their element. So much the better for hearing the rest of Harry's tale.

"If you remember back a day ago when I told you about my unexpected meeting with that stranger in Vienna..."

"Dr. Lucas Milton, if I recall correctly?" interrupted Julia.

"Exactly. He gave me a lot to think about on that day but one thing he told me stuck out like a pin on a cushion. He claimed that the Eemian relics are handed down from trustee to trustee over generations. And, he said, they had been that way for the last five thousand generations."

"Who are these trustees, ma'am," asked Grimes.

"Great question, John. Exactly what I was asking myself. And here's where it gets interesting."

The group leaned in towards Harry.

"Within a few weeks of meeting this Milton character, I stumbled upon another professor, this time at a climate conference in San Francisco. After a long day of speakers and conferences, we were getting to know the others over cocktails. I think I was sipping a glass of Prosecco when an older woman—had to be near 90 years old—asked me if I knew a Dr. Milton."

"Ok," said Sam, "this is definitely getting weird."

"Indeed," said Harry. "At first, I didn't make the connection but then she prompted me. Train station. Vienna.

"This was too specific to be a coincidence. It was as if she had been at that chance meeting. I drained my glass and then she and I went over to a quiet area of the hotel and found a table where we could sit at and talk. I definitely needed another drink but switched to water instead. This was suddenly getting very interesting."

Sky put his head on Julia's lap and she gently rubbed the fur between his ears.

"She seemed to know everything: the trip to Chile with Karl, the graphene tablet we found, the smuggling of the artifact, the strange language, and the bit about trustees of these ancient secrets held by the Eemians. Everything.

"I was spellbound as she elaborated on the story Dr. Milton told me. She went into some depth about the ancient legend, The Light and the end of the world.

"She explained that, 100,000 years ago, the Eemians split into two distinct groups, Quondans and Sahu, each opposed to the other. Sahu attacked Quondans, stole their secrets, and drove the survivors into hiding. It was the Quondans who built and occupied the sanctuaries, trying to keep their technology and hopes for the planet alive, while the Sahu weathered the next 90,000 years or so in caves. Both groups wanted the technology—the Quondans to save the planet from a second climate collapse, and the Sahu to destroy it and everything Quondan, because they believed it was Quondan technology that had driven them back into the Stone Age."

"And you believed all this?" Julia was struggling to control her voice, to limit her tone to one of rational skepticism, and not to sound dismissive or contemptuous. It wasn't quite working.

Harry was silent a long time, staring out the aircraft window. Finally, she answered.

"I do now. Yes. But back then? It took a lot of soul searching and a lot of faith. And faith is something that doesn't come easily to me. I'm a scientist—facts, figures, evidence are what rule my life as I am certain they do yours. Faith is for others I told myself. Yet I couldn't deny the evidence in my hands. I couldn't just whisk away the graphene tablet Karl and I had found." She ran her fingers through her hair.

"According to her, the descendants of both camps are still fighting this ancient feud, though now the Sahu call themselves the Sons of Nephilim, a group that want to bring about the Rapture, which they believe is inevitable."

"Uzziel," growled Grimes. "Sons of Nephilim...I hope I get another shot at him."

"Yes, John," said Harry, "and unfortunately, they are but one of several factions hell bent on civilization's destruction. But, fortunately, the Quondans are still working to save the planet."

"How?" asked Sam.

"According to her story, the Quondans emerged from their sanctuaries some 10,000 years ago. We see evidence of their guidance throughout civilization's history. The wheel. Agriculture. The pyramids. In the Middle Ages they were largely responsible for lifting society out of one of its darkest periods. They provided the light of education and wisdom. They built libraries, helped guide the world away from ignorance with science and the Enlightenment. Over the millennia, members have included Pythagoras, Ptolemy, Locke, Voltaire, and the Freemasons. They believe only by working to improve the lives of every human on the planet, along with being stewards of Earth's well-being, will humans survive. They do not want history to repeat itself. Today, the Quondans include some of the brightest, wealthiest individuals in the world."

"I am struggling here," said Julia. "This whole business is.."

"Hard to believe?" Interrupted Harry. "The three of you at least have the advantage of knowing the Eemians are real. Sam was inside one of their sanctuaries. Imagine how difficult it was for me to swallow this whole yarn before Sam's discovery. The only proof I had was a piece of the tablet."

Sam nodded.

Harry leaned forward. "But back to my story. Turns out she too was from UT Dallas, and, over the next few months, she began introducing me to people she claimed were Quondan descendants at the university and in the local community."

"What?" said Julia.

"I know. Crazy, right? These were some of the trustees of the Eemian legend. Some of these are people I know and respect and would never have guessed were part of a group like this one."

"And they're interested in this fusion stuff?" asked Grimes.

"More than just interested, John. More accurately, they're heavily invested. Or, I should say, *we* are heavily invested."

"My head is spinning," said Grimes.

"I understand, John. Believe me. But there's more."

All eyes were on Harry.

"I am glad you are all sitting down. What I am about to tell you next is going to make the story I just shared pale in comparison."

"Oh boy..." said Julia.

"Over the last 10 years, the trustees have built a nuclear fusion research facility in Dallas where we have managed to get close to building a working reactor. The facility is called the International Fusion Development Complex, or IFDC."

"What?" asked Sam.

"I know...hard to believe. That facility is funded by the Eemian trustees from around the world. And our mission is to develop a working fusion reactor in an attempt to help save the planet from climate collapse. Right up until the moment when Sam found the Eemian artifact, we were completely stumped as to how to power the reactor. Now, with Sam's artifact in hand, we have a clue of how to move forward."

"Back up a minute here," said Julia. "you're a . . . a member? You're somehow connected with these trustees?" This time Julia didn't try to hide her disbelief.

"Well, not exactly." Harry paused. On her face was a strange combination of expressions, Sam thought: a mix of embarrassment and pride, and maybe a bit of shame. "I'm their leader."

5

Dallas, Texas

The Lord gave, and the Lord hath taken away. So it was written in the book of Job.

For Magnus Sawyer, CEO of Empire Oil, the trouble was that the good Lord in his wisdom had been doing a hell of a lot more taking than giving of late. Like Job before him, Magnus didn't want to question or condemn or complain. But he didn't want to lose his business, either. Not when he'd put so damn much into it.

Too much, came the critical voice of his dead father to torment him. *To say nothing of the fortune you've spent on divorces and debutantes and this damn ugly building.*

Satan had tested Job. For Magnus, that role was played by the memory of Henry Sawyer. *The great Henry Sawyer.* Henry Sawyer hadn't needed a glass tower, reaching for the sky, to proclaim his worth. He hadn't needed memberships to the right clubs, the right golf courses, the right fundraisers where he'd be expected to donate the right amounts. Henry Sawyer knocked, and the door opened every goddamned time.

When Magnus knocked, he found only debt collectors on the other side. And despite all the cleverness he and his CFO had employed over the last year or two, it was only a matter of time until the rest of the world knew what Magnus had been trying so desperately to hide from them.

Empire Oil was going under. Sooner rather than later. And it would take Magnus with it. He was the captain, after all. No one would save him a seat on the lifeboat; they'd all expect him to go down with the ship.

Never mind that the iceberg that had torn the latest wound in Empire's hull wasn't his fault. Never mind that his goddamned lookout had up and jumped over the side of the boat and thrown in his lot with the ice.

Your metaphors always did get muddled when you were in your cups, came Henry's chiding voice. *Are you Job or the captain of the Titanic, boy?*

Magnus scowled into the depths of his whiskey just as the ice cube floating within it cracked with enough force to spit liquor into his eye.

For days after Sam's expected return from Greenland, Magnus had waited for his prodigal son to appear, tail between his legs, begging for scraps. He didn't exactly prepare the fatted calf, but he was prepared to extend his hand—for a price. Sam had to know who was boss, after all.

But Sam didn't come. Not to the house; not to the office. Magnus worked his way through at least one bottle of Wild Turkey, and with every drink, his benevolence ebbed. When he heard that Sam had shown his face at Grimes's barbecue party—which Magnus had considered too far beneath him to attend—he threw a glass at the wall, only to have Mrs. Langham, his secretary, look at him like *he* was the naughty child.

Magnus had been at home when the call finally came. When Iceberg Sam ripped through the hull, tore up the bulkheads, doomed

Empire Oil to the deadly deep of a debt from which it couldn't return.

"What?" he'd snarled into the phone, already frustrated.

Magnus didn't recognize the voice on the other end of the line—probably a good thing, or he'd have shot the messenger for sure. He listened as the idiot stammered his way through a list of the crimes Sam and Grimes had committed. The equipment they'd stolen. The charges they'd rung up on his already stressed line of credit. They'd hired some kind of expensive aircraft and specialist pilots. And it was too late to do a single thing to stop them.

The good ship Empire was already halfway underwater. She'd break any minute, split right down the middle.

Magnus spat a curse and didn't give the messenger a chance to reply before he slammed the phone down. Hard. Then he pushed it off the side of his desk, reveling in the sound of its destruction.

Why not? Why the hell not? A phone's the least of what's been destroyed today.

Magnus stood with such explosive force that his chair tumbled to the floor with a crash. He pounded both fists on his desk. Once. Twice. He was lifting them for a third blow when his housekeeper, Juanita, peeked her head around the door.

"Everything okay in here?"

"No! Goddammit!" bellowed Magnus. "Everything is not okay!"

She retreated.

Magnus stomped around his study. Not only had he lost funds he didn't have and equipment he couldn't replace, he'd been robbed of his core drilling team. *Grimes, you traitorous son of a bitch.*

Magnus had always known that Sam didn't have the courage to step up and do what was right for the family. The boy had failure written all over him from day one. But Grimes? Forty years on the job. Forty years of paying that old Texan whatever he demanded.

Grimes was to blame.

Magnus paced, growling to himself. He had trusted Grimes to raise the boy, to make him an Empire man, and now the two of them had turned against him. Stolen from him. Destroyed his chances at resurrecting the company. If a loss of such epic—and personal—proportions came to light, no one would do business with him ever again.

This would not stand. Could not. *I'll get my pound of flesh.*

Magnus trembled so hard he fell to his knees. *I should pray for the Lord to strike them both down. Sinners. Thieves. Traitors. Make an example of them.*

But when he lifted his eyes to Heaven, Magnus didn't see the face of God. He saw the larger-than-life portrait of his daddy hanging on the wall. Magnus had never liked the picture. The eyes followed him. Judged him. Found him wanting.

Should've got rid of the damn thing years ago.

"You laughing, old man?" Magnus asked the picture.

Henry's painted smile mocked him, and though Magnus wanted nothing more than to rise and pull the thing from the wall, slash it to pieces, burn it and dance around the flames, he did nothing but curl over his aching knees and pray as he'd never prayed before.

And in his head, he heard his daddy's words.

Put your faith in tradition and your trust in God's wisdom.

Magnus nodded over hands folded in supplication.

And for the love of Jesus, boy, stop your blubbering and pull yourself together.

6

Palo Pinto Mountains, Texas, Thirty-Two Years Earlier

Some weeks after Magnus Sawyer and his father, Henry, planted Grandpa Will under a towering marble monument befitting a man of his standing, young Magnus found himself summoned.

His father wasn't a man for boardrooms; Henry Sawyer was a man's man, a salt-of-the-Earth, red-blooded American who felt the only work worth doing was done in the open air with his own two hands, as God intended. As such, he believed the only words worth speaking were the ones uttered from the back of a horse or camping under starlit skies. More than one city boy had come knocking on Henry's door only to find himself abruptly clinging in terror to the reins of a horse who needed no such guidance to navigate the paths Henry preferred.

Thankfully, Magnus knew how to ride. He wasn't the horseman his father was, but he could hold his own without embarrassing himself. On that day, the Colorado mountain air was crisp and cool, scented by spruce and pine. The horses trudged up the mountain trail, their riders rocking comfortably in their saddles.

Magnus patted Chico's dark mane as they followed Atlas, his father's tall, coal-black steed, up the path. Chico wasn't fast and he wasn't pretty, but he was steady as a stone and near as reliable. Around them, Indian paintbrush and bitterroot peeked through the patchy green of the forest floor. Aggie, the dog Magnus was pretty sure his father loved more than he'd ever loved his own child, ran ahead and then dashed back, her tail wagging like it was on fire.

The trail turned from soft dirt to hard granite, and the horses' hooves clattered as they climbed. Below the small summit, a raging stream echoed through a canyon; their mounts snorted in relief as they meandered downhill.

They tied the horses to a tree by a quiet bend in the stream. Magnus gathered wood, brushed and fed Atlas and Chico, then pitched their tent as Henry cooked a pot of beans flavored with the slab of Woody's Smokehouse bacon Aggie had been vying for since they'd arrived. Magnus had eaten many a fine, fancy meal in his day, but nothing beat bacon and beans simmered over an open fire. On that, at least, he and his father could always agree.

When dinner was ready, Henry clasped his hands in prayer and dropped to his knees in front of the fire. He closed his eyes only once Magnus mirrored him.

"Lord, thank you for this bounty. Give me strength when I am weak, courage when I am afraid, wisdom when I am foolish, comfort when I am alone, hope in the face of rejection, and peace when I am in turmoil. Amen."

"Amen," echoed Magnus.

They ate in silence. When they were full to bursting, Henry let Aggie devour the scraps left in his bowl. Magnus cleaned the dishes, packed them up again, and sat quietly in the flickering light of the campfire, waiting for his father to take the stage.

Henry's summons always involved speeches.

"One of these days you're going to be running things, son."

Aggie curled at Henry's side, watching Magnus with eyes nearly as all-knowing as her master's. Magnus tried not to squirm beneath the scrutiny.

"I'm not sure you got the bit in your teeth just yet," he said, adding more wood to the fire. The flames licked hungrily at the fuel. Henry shook his head. "You still hesitate too much." He cast his son a sideling glance. "People respect decisiveness in a man."

Magnus opened his mouth to answer, but the horses whinnied; he and Aggie looked up at the noise. Their little fire cast shadows that jumped and flickered in the inky night. Even the horses' silhouettes seemed to dance.

"I ... I'll work on it, sir," Magnus said. He tried to sound decisive. He wasn't sure he succeeded.

Henry furrowed his brow. "Magnus."

"Yes, sir?"

The silence the followed was punctuated only with the sounds of the fire and nature around them. Far away, a coyote howled. A second or two later, another answered. "Are you afraid of me, son?"

How am I supposed to answer that? Magnus swallowed hard. *What can I say?* Henry Sawyer didn't suffer fools lightly, and he didn't believe in handling anyone with kid gloves. Including his son.

The fire popped suddenly and threw sparks at their feet. Embers burned brightly before dimming and dying. An owl's screech echoed through the canyon. The dog crept closer to the tents, and Magnus pulled his collar close. He didn't want to sit silent as a bump on a log, but he wasn't sure how to answer.

More to the point, he didn't know what his father wanted to *hear.*

Henry shrugged, clearly having taken Magnus's silence as an affirmative. "I s'pose I've been rough on you." He tossed a small pinecone into the flames. It erupted in a fountain of sparks. "Your Grandpa Will, God rest his soul, didn't believe in going easy on folks either. Certainly not me. 'Treat 'em soft,' he'd say, 'and they melt at the first hint of trouble.'"

Father and son stared into the flames.

"You can't be soft, boy. You can't melt at the first sign of trouble.

That's not going to work around Empire. The crew needs a leader. A man with a strong hand on the tiller."

Magnus nodded, trying to radiate certainty. In truth, he'd never tilled an inch of land in the whole of his life and couldn't begin to imagine what that kind of strong hand would be like. "Yes, sir."

Henry Sawyer's eyes narrowed. Magnus met the gaze as long as he dared, but he felt his father peeling back every layer, exposing every flaw, every weakness. Magnus looked back to the fire, eyes beginning to water. If his father remarked on it, he'd just say the campfire smoke was stinging them.

Aggie rose and paced before settling at Magnus's side, planting her head on his thigh. Magnus rested one hand on the dog's warm head, stroking her soft ears.

"This is man's work, son. It's hard, but that's true of all good work. God gave you two hands and strength enough to use them. I know you'll pull it together and make me proud. You're a Sawyer."

As Magnus stroked Aggie's head, he looked past the campfire toward the stream, where the water lapped softly against the rocks. The reflected moonlight was like liquid silver. In the shadows, Chico and Atlas stood side by side, grazing like old friends. The wind was changing. Clouds moving in.

"Now, I don't expect to be going anywhere for a good long time. We Sawyers are made of tougher stock than that."

A light rain began to fall. Aggie nudged her muzzle under Magnus's hand, and he realized he'd stopped scratching her ears.

"Someday it'll all be up to you, and you need to be ready for that. Times are changing. There's even talk about a new way of drilling. Horizontal." Henry spat on the ground. "Damnedest thing I ever heard of."

"You mean fracking?"

"I don't know what they call it, son, but whatever it is, it sounds like something made up by the devil himself. These high-tech oil drillers are going to ruin our industry. You mark my words."

The light, misting rain turned colder. Fall was coming, and with it, the snows that would bury the forest colors in a blanket of unending white.

Henry stood, brushing the grass and ash from his pants before stretching his arms high above his head. "'Bout time I hit the sack. I'll see you bright and early. We gotta get back to Dallas." He ducked into the tent, and within a few minutes, low snoring came rumbling out.

Magnus didn't immediately follow. With Aggie warm at his side, he sat in the misty dark and wondered who he might have been in a world where he hadn't been born an Empire Sawyer.

But what's the point of trying to imagine that?

The mist soaked into his clothes, leaving Magnus wet, cold, and miserable. *I'm just an idiot,* he thought darkly to himself. *Gotta stop that.* He could be the type of son his father wanted. He could be. He just had to try harder.

Magnus stood and tended the fire before climbing into the tent and wriggling into his sleeping bag. Aggie lay between Magnus and his father.

Some people had choices, and others had choices made for them.

No question which camp Magnus belonged to.

7

Dallas, Texas

Sam couldn't quite wrap his head around it.

"You're telling me the International Fusion Development Complex," Sam mused, "is in ... a mall?" Sunlight pushed through the skylights, illuminating the broad, empty area. Once upon a time, it might have been slated to be a food court. Now it was a pristine foyer, revealing nothing remotely suspect about what they'd find inside.

"We're borrowing from nature," Harry replied as they walked through the cavernous entryway. "After a fashion. Hiding in plain sight is the best camouflage, remember. Think of us as a giant hermit crab."

Sky trotted ahead before making a wide circle back around to Sam's side.

"What if someone decides to buy the property?" Julia asked.

Harry shook her head. "Oh, the property's bought and paid for.

Anyone decides they want to develop it, they'll get a whole lot of runaround and decide this place isn't worth the effort."

"You hope, anyway," Sam said.

"Darn right I hope so," she replied on a chuckle. "It takes a lot of money to keep this place up to code ... while also making it look like a hot mess nobody wants to touch."

Harry led them to a glass-paneled railing that formed an enormous ring broken only by frozen escalators.

From that spot, they looked down on as much of the IFDC as they could see. A maze of shining metal and sleek black computer equipment snaked this way and that. Simulations ran on huge computer screens in one section, while in another, holographic representations of artifacts hovered midair.

"We considered using one of the basement levels," Harry said, "since the building has several. But the airflow was terrible. The electronics ran too hot. The physics labs and our servers had to be separated and outfitted with special cooling equipment. Down that way," she said with a gesture, "are the physics labs." She jerked her thumb in the opposite direction. "Down the other, you'll find our machine learning and artificial intelligence team."

Far removed from the barely controlled chaos was what looked like a library, with shelves upon shelves of books spanning from floor to ceiling, and long tables crowded with paper notebooks and laptop computers.

"What's back there?" Julia asked, pointing.

"The linguistics and translation teams," Harry said. "Brilliant people, but a little odd."

"In what way?" Sam asked.

"They're very ... *analog.*" She said the word like it described something communicable.

Julia chuckled. "I'd have figured you'd appreciate that quality."

Harry gave a little *hmph.* "You can learn from the past without emulating it."

As they explored, Sky stuck close by, if not by Sam's side, then by Julia's. His nose worked furiously as he scented the air, and he held his curled tail high, like a question mark indicating his curiosity.

You aren't the only one, buddy, Sam thought. He tried not to gape, but it was too much to take in at once. Everything battled for his attention, from screens flashing equations and compiling code to the unfinished holographic projection reconstructing the Eemian pyramid in Antarctica. Several workstations over, three scientists argued over what appeared to be a dire climate simulation.

The atmosphere was tense but determined.

Hard work is its own reward.

It wasn't a party. Nobody was having fun down here, but everyone was wholly engrossed in their task.

Sam wanted to join them. He wanted it deep down in his bones.

Harry led the way through the labyrinth of workstations, stopping when they reached a cluster of researchers who looked to be undergraduates. "Allow me to introduce the future of the IFDC." Harry rattled off introductions with ease that made Sam wonder if the group came from Harry's classes. He offered a smile and wave to the group before sneaking a look at Julia. *I'll see if she retained any of that later.*

"These bright minds ready to tackle just about anything we throw at them—including you two," Harry said, grinning. "Everyone's excited for you to join the team."

Sam chuckled. "Are you saying our reputations precede us, Doc?"

Harry's smile didn't waver. "You'd better believe they do." She checked her watch and nodded. "Speaking of which, I'd say it's high time we had some proper introductions, don't you?"

Julia nudged Sam with her elbow. "Take notes, Dr. Sawyer," she said in a stage whisper. "There'll be a pop quiz later."

They followed Harry further away from the noise and chaos of the workstations. En route to the conference room, they passed through a gallery. Glass cases displayed ancient manuscripts, pieces of pottery, and rough-hewn tools from another age.

"What's all this?" Sam asked.

"My private collection. If I'm going to spend more time here than I do at my own home, I might as well bring a few of my favorite things, right?" She smiled fondly at each item, safe behind glass. "It's always fascinated me, you know. The history of early man, cultural advancements through generations." Harry shrugged. "It's a nice little reminder of what we're working toward—uncovering those mysteries."

8

The IFDC's primary conference area was a rotunda at the furthest end of the mall's ground floor. Soundproof glass separated the conference hall from the rest of the labs and workstations. Despite being headquartered in a derelict, unfinished mall, nothing about the IFDC's interior resembled anything related to retail.

The ceiling's acoustic paneling allowed every speaker to be heard, and with enormous screens ringing the room, not a single iota of information would go unseen. Circular five-top tables filled the body of the room, each equipped with built-in USB hubs, allowing for ease of movement between presenters. At one end of the hall was a large, curved oak table. Harry currently sat behind it, with Sam and Julia on either side. Sky lay under the table, head resting heavily on one of Sam's feet.

"Good morning, everyone." Harry paused and glanced at her watch. "Yes, still morning for a little longer. I realize you all have work to do, so thank you for taking time out of your schedules to meet here." She gave the room one of her trademark grins. "I promise it'll be worth it."

A few heads bent together as they whispered back and forth.

"I know you've all read the reports, so I won't bore everyone—or embarrass these two—with a long prelude. May I introduce Dr. Julia Bassi and Dr. Sam Sawyer." She paused. "And in case anyone *didn't* read those reports, Dr. Bassi was instrumental in locating the Antarctica site, while Dr. Sawyer and the late Dr. Karl Satsky ventured inside."

Murmurs rippled across the room; once all was quiet again, Harry went on. "You know about their escape from the Eemian pyramid buried under approximately a half-mile of Antarctic ice. Drs. Sawyer and Bassi's ability to keep their wits about them under immense pressure, to say nothing of their wealth of knowledge and varied experience, make them invaluable additions to the IFDC team."

Another rustle of noise came and went.

Harry inclined her head slightly. "With a few exceptions, the IFDC has been focusing on solving the problem of fusion in order to address the energy crisis and the effect our use of fossil fuels has had on the Earth's climate. In that quest we've reached an impasse. How do we feed the fusion reactor. Thanks to Dr. Sawyer's discovery of metalized hydrogen inside the Eemian pyramid, we now know part of the answer. And, we believe, the answers to the remaining questions are buried inside the remaining Eemian sanctuaries."

Harry tapped a keyboard in front of her, and the screens around the room came to life, each showing a different image—photos of artifacts, as well Sam's photos from within the pyramid.

"Moving forward, the IFDC will dedicate its resources and manpower to uncovering the mysteries of Quondan technology so that we may complete our work on building a working fusion reactor. I have every reason to believe that their Power of the Light was, in fact, a fusion generator."

The ensuing silence was thick—though with skepticism, anticipation, or something less definable, Sam wasn't sure.

"It is my firm belief," Harry said, "that these mysteries can be uncovered, and these secrets can absolutely be unlocked and used to our advantage. Anyone who can't get on that particular wagon might as well leave the room right now."

Nobody left.

"I'm not saying it'll be easy, and I'm not saying it'll be quickly done. But if any group of people in the world is up to the task, it's you. Everyone in this room brings different knowledge, skillsets, and talents to the task ahead. If we work together, I have no doubt we'll succeed."

A round of applause followed.

"Team leads, let's have some introductions."

One person from each table rose to their feet.

Harry gestured to her right. "We'll start with you, Francois. Would you mind saying a few words?"

A tall, slender man with short, disheveled, auburn hair offered a little wave. His glasses gave him an owlish look offset only by the green and yellow Hawaiian-print necktie he wore, its knot hopelessly loosened. When he spoke, his voice was deep, resonating with a Parisian accent.

"I am Francois Severeaux. My team handles machine learning and artificial intelligence. *Enchanté.*" He bowed at the waist and, as he took his seat again, seemed relieved to be out of the spotlight.

"Not so fast, Francois," Harry said. Francois startled slightly and rose again.

"Ah ... *Oui, professeure?*"

Harry looked at both Sam and Julia. "Francois is being modest. Exceptionally so. The IFDC would grind to an absolute halt without Fran and his team."

Francois turned pink to the tips of his ears, and Sam felt a pang of sympathy for the man.

"*Merci,*" he said, and sat before Harry could stop him a second time.

At the next table, the team lead was Severeaux's absolute opposite —sartorially speaking, at least. He needed no prompting from Harry to begin speaking. His clipped accent formed vowels with perfect Oxbridge precision.

"Dr. James Worthington-Carver." The tailored suit oozed elegance, and Sam had never seen anything like the elaborate knot in which the man had formed his tie. "History. My specialty is ancient civilizations—the same is true of nearly my entire team. Among other things, we provide the reminder that knowing the past is vital to shaping the future."

"Else you repeat it," Julia said.

James nodded briefly. "Precisely."

"More importantly," Harry said, "if you want a proper cuppa, see James."

After Dr. Worthington-Carver sat, conversation rippled at the next table. After some discussion, a Hispanic woman stood, her dark hair pulled into a braid hanging nearly to her waist. She wore chinos and a vibrant orange sweater. Smiling shyly, she gave Harry a quick wave.

"Dr. Marisol Gutierrez, interim team lead, cartography," she said.

Harry snapped her fingers. "That's right—Reg's out of the country. Nearly slipped my mind. Sorry to put you on the spot, Mari."

"I can tolerate the spotlight for a few minutes. He's due back tonight, at any rate," Marisol replied, before smiling at Sam and Julia. "Dr. Mountbatten's specialization is cartography; mine, however, is photogrammetry." Her smile tilted into a grin. "You'll find those two specialties in varying degrees among our team members."

"You'll definitely want to get to know Dr. Gutierrez," Harry told Julia. "She's also our resident coffee snob."

Marisol inclined her head. "It's not snobbery to appreciate quality."

As Dr. Gutierrez sat, the woman at the next table stepped forward. She was tiny; she couldn't have been much taller than five feet even. She dressed casually, in a plain navy dress and white tennis shoes. As she spoke, she rolled to the balls of her feet and back again, brunette curls bouncing with every movement. "Dr. Betty Faulkner, linguistics," she said in a loud, clear voice tinged with a Boston accent. "Pleasure's mine, naturally. Dr. Bickford has had us—my team, I mean, and myself, of course—working on decoding the Quondan language, which has been absolutely fascinating." Dr. Faulkner spoke rapidly, but each word was crisply enunciated. "It's not quite a standard alphabet like the Phoenician—a bit more like cuneiform, but only loosely. The goal, obviously, is to get a reliable translation program working." She smiled broadly and clasped her hands together. "*Monsieur* Severeux has been a huge help on that end."

Harry hid her chuckle in a cough. "Sam, Julia, please welcome Dr. Faulkner. Be gentle, she's shy."

Dr. Faulkner let out a loud *ha* and sat.

As if emboldened by Dr. Faulkner, the next team lead took a step forward, away from her chair. She was nearly the same height as Dr. Worthington-Carver, blond and athletic, wearing classic black trousers and an emerald sweater. "Lily Harrington," she said, her words free of any evident regional accent. "I lead the cryptography team."

"Lily has a knack for unraveling tricky codes, which I am confident will come in handy later down the line. Deciphering the language is just part of the puzzle," Harry explained. "And, last but not least, Dr. Dai-Lu Chen."

Dr. Chen looked up at Harry, her face etched with deep lines, and she smiled.

"Dr. Chen is a master in physics and will provide essential knowledge about the Eemians' technological advances as they pertain to fusion."

"You flatter me, Dr. Bickford," said Dr. Chen.

"I'm no flatterer," Harry replied. "Any compliments I give are earned."

"Our team will unravel the mysteries of metalized hydrogen," Dr. Chen said simply. "So that we may make full use of this technology."

Harry looked between Sam and Julia, smiling. "These people are the best of the best." Her smile tightened and she blinked rapidly. "Karl would be beside himself." She sniffled and brushed at her eyes. "Well. He'd be thrilled ... or pissed he hadn't done it first."

9

Dallas, Texas

The air shimmered with humidity as Magnus gazed up at the twelve-story Dallas Park Center. The imposing edifice of silvery-blue reflective glass and brush-finished stainless-steel spandrels was the very image of success.

Or at least it had been, back when he'd poured so much of his dead father's money into building it.

There it is, Henry, Magnus thought. *You son of a bitch. When they think of Empire Oil, this is what they picture.*

Magnus hung his head. *I don't know how much longer I can keep up this game.* The distant cheers of a soccer crowd echoed across the street in Lee Park as he walked past a line of leafing oak trees toward the plaza that welcomed visitors to the Center.

"Morning, Mr. Sawyer."

Magnus kept his head down as he greeted the security officer who seemed forever ensconced in his solitary cubicle, surrounded by video monitors beaming images from the building's different floors.

The sound of Magnus's bespoke shoes striking marble echoed through the cavernous lobby as he made his way to the elevator and the top floor.

"Good morning, sir." Mrs. Langham's flat tone hadn't changed in more than thirty years.

"Have there been any calls?"

Do they know? Does everyone know?

"A few, but Mr. Havens is staving them off. I ... I don't think it's common knowledge quite yet."

"Charlie's a good CFO, but he's not God," said Magnus.

"He has his ways." The scowl permanently chiseled into Mrs. Langham's face cracked briefly into the weakest of smiles. "Here's the mail." She stuffed a pile of white envelopes into Magnus's hands as they reached the tall, dark-walnut double doors of his office.

Magnus sighed as strode to his desk, the same dark wooden fixture from which his father had commanded Empire Oil once upon a time, in a much humbler building. The desk didn't match the exterior of the Dallas Park Center, but he'd needed to claim it. He threw the envelopes onto the piles of paper already amassed on the varnished wooden surface.

My father would have fixed our problems with the snap of his fingers. Magnus winced as he imagined the inevitable tirade of shame and disappointment that would have followed.

Henry had subscribed to the idea that the more he reminded his son of his weaknesses, the harder Magnus would work to strengthen himself. Instead, he'd only succeeded in beating Magnus down, breaking him without building him back up again. Magnus had never lived up to his father's expectations. The more he failed, the weaker he seemed to become.

The only time Magnus had ever seen the old man pleased was the day he put a squalling Samuel Henry Magnus Sawyer in his arms.

What a goddamned shame that Sam had been disappointing Magnus ever since.

Magnus had found a peculiar kind of solace in successfully side-stepping any and all responsibilities that might test his mettle—a tactic that had served him well until Henry's sudden death. His father had hit the floor, still clutching his chest, not three paces from the desk where Magnus now sat—albeit in the much smaller, humbler building from which Henry had run Empire Oil. Even now, all these years later, Magnus remembered the unholy sense of joy that had washed over him, like a weight lifting from his shoulders, as he watched the paramedics pull the sheet over Henry's stone-gray face. That sense of joy still haunted Magnus more than thirty years later. His final sin against his father. The one for which he could never atone. Didn't want to atone.

Through the large rectangular windows that formed the wall of his office, wavy lines of thick morning heat shimmered off the cement walks and black asphalt roads below.

"It's gonna be a hot one," he said.

"Looks like it, sir." Mrs. Langham made a space on the cluttered surface of the desk for the cup of coffee she was holding. She stood still for a moment before dragging a chair from the other side of the room to his desk and grabbing a few of the papers.

"Time to rob Peter to pay Paul," she said, evidently trying to add a little levity. He wished he could laugh.

Magnus cleared his throat. "One hundred and fifty dollars. That's how much we got for a barrel just five years ago."

"I know, sir."

"Fracking, Mrs. Langham. Fracking. Oil and gas trapped in shale. It was our future." Sam was supposed to be the future. *And look how that's gone. Thief. Traitor.*

"You couldn't have known."

"Canada and Russia—and oh, hell, everyone else—had to come in for a piece of the pie. And those greedy OPEC assholes keep upping their production. Got their sandaled feet on our goddamned necks."

Mrs. Langham lowered her head.

"Not to mention those fool environmentalists with their 'tainted water supply' and 'methane in the air' bullshit." Magnus shook his head. "And my crazy son is one of them. He should've killed me outright. Would've been kinder than this."

Magnus turned around as Mrs. Langham ran a hand over the documents in her lap. "Maybe I should come back—"

"All of them, all of *them* are to blame." His face burned with heat, as if newly sunburned. "I should still own this building. I built it. *I did.* Not him. Not them. But all those motherfuckers—"

Mrs. Langham cleared her throat meaningfully.

"I'm sorry, Janet," said Magnus. "It's just that—"

"Maybe let's meet back after lunch." Mrs. Langham got up from her chair, placed the papers in her hand on the corner of the desk, and shut the office doors on her way out.

"Dammit," he whispered.

He reached into the desk's single locked drawer and probed for the cool metal inside. The tips of his fingers traced the engraving upon its surface: S&W .357 MAGNUM.

Insurance.

If push came to shove, he wasn't going to drown slowly with his broken ship. No, sir. They wouldn't drag Magnus Henry Sawyer in front of the cameras to weep and bemoan his fate like a woman or a child.

Mrs. Langham's muffled voice drifted to his ears. "I'm not sure when he'll be available. Perhaps you'd like to talk to our CFO?"

As his knees started to shake, Magnus closed the drawer. On silent feet, he headed toward Mrs. Langham's voice. His fingers fumbled for his office door's worn deadbolt and, after securing it, his sweating hands slid down the dark wood until his knees hit the floor and his palms fell to his chest.

Magnus squeezed his eyes shut and did his best to clear his mind, but he couldn't banish the image of Henry's face in the last few moments of his life. Magnus had watched his father die, seen him fall. They'd been talking. Actually, Henry had been shouting, threatening to take Empire Oil away from Magnus and sell it "Before you have a chance to fuck it up." Henry had risen from his leather chair, intent on calling his attorney, but hadn't made it more than few steps before falling on his face. Magnus had frozen, hopeful yet afraid, terrified that Henry might not get up ... and terrified that he would.

He'd looked at the phone on his father's desk and known he should call for help. Still, his body wouldn't move. An eternity later, he managed to roll his father onto his back. Henry's eyelids were open, as if he'd seen something horrifying, and his mouth was twisted mid-scream. Magnus had stood and stumbled backward, shocked at his expression. With the toe of his boot, Magnus nudged his father's prone body.

Only then had he reached for the phone.

The past and the present seemed to merge. Magnus's palms were pressed so tightly together that his chest muscles hurt, and he was afraid that if he opened his eyes, he'd see his dead father once again crumpled on the floor. He pleaded with his God for help and tried to calm his fears—fears that he had spent his life hiding from others.

God wore Henry's face.

Magnus's minister had often counseled him with the words of the apostle James: "Yet even when you pray, your prayers are not answered, because you pray just for selfish reasons."

Though his pleas were selfish, Magnus hoped God wouldn't notice. Hadn't James also written in his epistle: "When you ask for something you must have faith and not doubt"?

Trouble was, Magnus had both faith *and* doubt. He struggled up from the floor, took a deep breath, and returned to his desk.

The chair groaned as he slumped into it. On his shiny wooden desk sat a folder labeled IRS. Magnus set it atop another stack and lined it up perfectly with the folders beneath it.

He opened the desk drawer, wrapped his palm around the blue steel cradled within it, and lifted the handgun from the drawer, carefully placing it atop his desk. Curious. He had never noticed the mirror image of the desktop's finish before. With his index finger, he stroked the pistol's knurled handle, admiring the precision of its crosshatch pattern.

His father's gun, gifted to him on his twenty-first birthday.

Everything Magnus owned had first belonged to Henry. Except this building. And soon it, too, would be taken.

Magnus cradled the gun in both hands.

You don't have the guts, boy. Never did.

Magnus opened his liquor cabinet and set the gun next to the glassware. He pulled an unopened bottle of Russell's Reserve Wild Turkey Bourbon from the row. Seemed appropriate; the distillers were father and son.

Magnus pulled a shot glass from the top shelf, examined it for cleanliness, then filled it. He lifted the bourbon to his nose for a deep inhale before emptying it into his waiting mouth and swishing the burning liquid across his tongue before swallowing. His eyes watered. He set the glass on the counter and picked up the gun. Its heft and coolness reassured him.

Insurance. The insurance that couldn't fail.

The bourbon calmed his fast-beating heart, and a welcome serenity washed over him. His father would be proud. Finally. He returned to his desk and opened the pistol's cylinder, exposing six rounds, each with a copper-colored blunt tip. He angled the pistol enough to slide out one of the bullets. He placed the cartridge back into the cylinder and locked it shut. He gently pulled back the hammer with his thumb until it made a satisfying click. Magnus closed his eyes and reveled in the cold assurance of the trigger's steel against his index finger.

10

The ringing phone startled Magnus. He pulled himself out of his trance and carefully lowered the hammer of the gun still clutched in his sweaty palm.

"Yes?" he said into the receiver, his voice hoarse.

"Sir," said Mrs. Langham, "it's him again."

"Him?" asked Magnus, weary of all the hims and thems on his tail. Only a matter of time until they tore him to shreds.

"Yes, sir. He's been coming every week with a proposal. He says it'll only take a few minutes. Shall I send him away again?"

Magnus returned the gun to its drawer. His father had been right. He wasn't man enough to handle this. Neither was his son—the coward, the goddamn thief.

"Tell him he has ten minutes," Magnus barked into the phone. "And if he stays any longer, alert security and have him removed."

The tall double doors to Magnus's office opened inward after Mrs. Langham's key unlocked them.

"Sir, this is Dr. Ethan Pickens."

Ethan Pickens was rail-thin, almost gaunt. In his hand was a briefcase of weathered brown leather. He stood at stiff attention just inside the entrance to Magnus's office.

Magnus caught Mrs. Langham's eye, and she nodded her understanding that this visitor would be leaving in exactly ten minutes. Maybe less. She closed the doors behind herself. Ethan Pickens remained just inside the office. His gray hair was plastered over the middle of his bony head in a vain attempt to cover his bald spot, but it did little to distract the eye from his enormous beak of a nose.

"Pickens." Magnus moved toward the long glass table and took a seat. "I'm told you have a proposal. I'm a busy man. Make it quick."

Pickens held onto the briefcase with his left hand, and with his right, reached over and undid the straps. From within, he pulled an old-fashioned alarm clock topped with twin bells. He set the device down, facing Magnus.

"Sir, if what I reveal in the next ten minutes doesn't intrigue you, I will leave your office and never return. Is that fair?"

Magnus nodded his acceptance.

"Thank you, sir." Pickens clicked a switch on the rear of the clock and its ticking filled the quiet room.

Pickens pulled aside the chair closest to Magnus. Instead of sitting, he stood in its place and set his briefcase on the table.

"You're a man of vision, Mr. Sawyer. For decades, your family's been on the cutting edge of the oil business. I have no doubt that you are wise enough to invest in the future."

Magnus's eyes never wavered from Pickens's Ichabod Crane face. *This guy's either clueless or delusional.* Not that it mattered which; Mrs. Langham would soon escort this unwelcome scarecrow out the door.

From inside his cracked leather case, Pickens retrieved two folded pieces of paper. He reached over the desk and unfolded one in front of Magnus.

"Look familiar?"

Magnus looked down at a contour map. Imprinted over its green background were layers of sideways figure-eight shapes of differing colors: the smallest inner shape was red, then dark blue, growing to light blue. The largest was green. As he peered closer, lamenting the pride that kept him from wearing the reading glasses he needed, he saw numbers at different points within the colored shapes: 4200, 4400, 4390.

Magnus knew what it was. A map of formation tops observed in multiple petroleum well logs, displaying their height relative to the terrain and each other.

"Now, sir," said Pickens. He leaned over the desk and unfolded a second sheet of paper atop the first. "I'm sure you've seen your share of pay maps?"

Magnus knew full well the meaning of a pay map—a simple overlay of the contour map showing the potential yield or income from each wellhead.

Pickens pointed to one spot on the pay map. "Can you see the numbers there? I apologize for their small size."

Magnus perched his reading glasses atop the bridge of his nose. "Fifty MMCFD?" He tossed the paper back onto the desk. "Impossible."

"Fifty million cubic feet of natural gas per day." Pickens eyes seemed lit by a fervor that made Magnus want to squirm. "That's ten to twenty times the expected yield of a productive well. Yet not only is it possible, it is a fact. And that well is not more than fifty miles from your own well sites in Colorado."

Magnus's eyebrows raised. The man was definitely delusional ... but fifty million cubic feet a day? Yields like that could change everything.

Pickens craned his head to see the front of the alarm clock. "Looks like my time's nearly up, sir. Are you interested in hearing more?"

As if on cue, a knock on the door preceded the entrance of a green-suited security guard. He peeked his head around the edge of the door and tried to make eye contact with Magnus. The door opened wider, to admit Mrs. Langham.

Magnus tore his eyes away from the pay map on his desk. For a moment, he couldn't remember why Mrs. Langham was standing there.

"Sir," she interrupted. "You—"

"Not now, Mrs. Langham. I've granted Dr. Pickens another few minutes to explain himself and his ridiculous claims."

Mrs. Langham nodded, turned, and walked out the door, followed by the stone-faced security guard.

The industry expectations for natural gas well yields were one to two million cubic feet per day on the low side, three to five million on average. Gigantic wells could sometimes produce as much as twenty million cubic feet per day. This beanpole stranger claimed a single well next to Empire's Colorado property was producing more than *twice* that amount—more than all the wells owned by Empire combined.

"Now," said Magnus, "seems to me that you're trying to heap a load of horseshit on my desk and wasting my time to boot. Where's your proof?"

Pickens switched off the alarm clock, reached into his satchel, and pulled out a stapled stack of paper. He laid it on Magnus's desk.

"Please open to page twelve."

Magnus looked down his nose at Pickens before turning his attention to the document without touching it. Bold lettering on the front read:

DISCLAIMER

This report was prepared as an account of work sponsored by an agency of the United States Government. Neither the United States Government nor any agency thereof, nor any of their employees...

"What's the government got to do with this?" asked Magnus. "They don't measure well yields or produce reports like this."

Pickens reached over the desk and opened the document to page twelve, titled "Test Well Predicted Rate." Below that, a simple graph with its vertical Y axis showing a scale of zero through fifty, was labeled PRODUCTION: MMCFD.

"The date on the bottom of this page is 1969," growled Magnus.

"I can explain everything, if you'd like."

"If I'd like?" Magnus repeated. "You think I'm an idiot, Pickens? Fifty million cubic feet per day is an absurd number. Even in the worst times, wellhead pricing's been around three grand per million cubic feet. A hundred and fifty thousand dollars a day? Nearly five million a month? No one produces that. Nothing. Nowhere."

"I'm an engineer, not a salesman, and I'm not interested in wasting a minute of your time. Every word I've spoken is true, sir."

Magnus closed the document.

"Let's say for a moment that I believe you, which, frankly, I do not," said Magnus. "What's all this got to do with me? I'm an oil man. Empire only dabbles in natural gas."

"Your company has a hundred-year lease on acreage near this test well. Those Colorado gas wells of yours aren't producing anywhere near the revenues I can help you get."

Magnus glared at the man.

"Your family's built a great company around oil, but natural gas is the future. It's clean, it might help save the planet, and"—he winked—"I guarantee these numbers will make your investors smile."

Magnus was only glad the man said *investors* and not *debt collectors.* Maybe he didn't know. Maybe the news hadn't yet spread.

Pickens reached across the desk and retrieved the papers, returning them to his briefcase as a broad grin stretched his face.

"Look, Mr. Sawyer. Empire's land in Colorado is more valuable than you might imagine. It borders the Green River Formation—a group of intermountain lakes connected by the Green River through three states: Colorado, Utah, and Wyoming." Pickens paced in front of Magnus's conference table. "The Green River Formation contains more energy than any other place in the world." He stopped and leaned both hands on the table's edge. "Trapped deep in the shale is an estimated three *trillion* barrels of energy—that's trillion, sir, trillion with a T. It's the single largest energy deposit on the planet, bigger than what remains in the Middle East and all the oil used since the beginning of the Industrial Revolution, combined."

It was all Magnus could do to keep a straight face.

Pickens resumed pacing. "No one has been able to pull much

energy out of that area because of the limitations of hydraulic fracturing in deep wells and the environmental concerns regarding groundwater contamination. Most of the gas is trapped in vast areas that require deep, broad wells that are prohibitively expensive to drill and maintain. I have developed technology to extract that energy—one that is not only environmentally acceptable, but financially viable for a company the size of Empire."

"How?" demanded Magnus.

The engineer rose to his full height and folded his arms across his chest. "It's a secret, Mr. Sawyer. To find out, you'll have to travel with me to Colorado."

"You walk into my office with this crazy song and dance and expect me to get on a plane to find out what all this is about?" Magnus rose from his chair and gripped the edge of the table. "Do you take me for a fool?"

"No, sir. Not one little bit. But if I'm wasting your time ... "

Magnus silently watched the man's every move, searching for a weakness. A tell. Nothing. Either Pickens was telling God's honest truth, or this was a game of poker Magnus was doomed to lose in a big way.

He cast a swift glance at the drawer that held his gun. *How much do I have left to lose, anyway?* "Hold your horses, there, Pickens. If this plan of yours holds water, you won't mind me getting a little expert advice. Maybe bringing a little of that expert advice with me on our fieldtrip to the Centennial State?"

Pickens inclined his head. "By all means. All I ask is that you ... choose that advice wisely. Someone, say, with your best interests at heart. If the wrong person catches wind of this—"

Magnus waved a dismissive hand. "Pickens, you're bringing me papers from 1969. You've been showing up and getting turned away for weeks, Mrs. Langham says. You can give me a day or two to check your references."

Pickens didn't quite smile, but he nodded. "Of course, sir. I'd expect no less."

11

Dallas, Texas

The sun had just begun to rise, turning the night sky to a silvery-blue hue, as Magnus gazed out the window of his office at home. He hadn't slept a wink, and the bottle of bourbon on his bedside table was untouched. Over and over, he saw those maps Pickens had laid out before him. Over and over, he imagined how even a fraction of that money could save his hide. More than that. It could make Empire great again. A legacy he could be proud of. A legacy, he thought, that even his father would have to approve of.

This kingdom, this empire of oil and gas, was his responsibility. He had spent his whole life trying to make it a success. Mostly, he had to admit, he'd failed. He could almost feel the weight of the gun in his hand, but it was safely locked away. For now.

Pickens's proposal was a risk. Outright madness, some would say. Probably his damned investors. Magnus sighed heavily, his mind racing with the possibilities and the possible failure that could come from this decision. He had spent the last few hours contemplating how to approach the challenge, but now he was exhausted and completely overwhelmed.

Desperately, he knelt and began to pray. He asked for guidance and begged God to help him make the right decision. When he closed his eyes, a peace that he hadn't felt for a long time washed over him.

A loud knock reverberated through the room. Magnus's eyes snapped open, and he jumped to his feet. The door opened slowly, revealing the all-too-familiar frame of John Grimes. At first, Magnus thought he must be dreaming, must have fallen asleep mid-prayer. And then his anger ignited like tinder in a forest fire, a volatile and unpredictable force that threatened to consume everything in its path.

If the gun had been in Magnus's hand right now, he sure as hell wouldn't have turned it on himself.

"Sir," Grimes said. "You have every right to turn me away, but I-I hope you'll hear me out."

"The only thing I want to hear is how you plan to repay everything you stole, John Grimes. After everything I've done for you. Everything this *company* has done for you."

Grimes spread his hands wide. Wide and empty.

Magnus was reaching for the phone to call the police when a flash of sunlight on the horizon caught something reflective outside, nearly blinding him. His knees still ached with all the praying he'd done.

He took a deep breath and looked at Grimes. Anger still pulsed through his veins, but he pushed it down. "If you want to come home," he said, "you'll have to prove your loyalty." He paused and looked Grimes in the eye. "If you put one toe out of line, it will be Sam who takes the punishment. Do you understand?"

Grimes nodded. "Yes, sir."

A wave of relief washed over Magnus as his anger started to subside. "Good," he said. "Pack your bags. We have a plane to catch this afternoon."

Grimes didn't push. Didn't even ask where they were headed. *Good man.*

Magnus looked out the window once more, watching the sky lighten. Grimes would know what to do about Pickens. He'd know the questions that needed asking. And one way or another, he would repay the debt he owed.

12

Grand Mesa, Colorado

Dr. Ethan Pickens slowed the SUV and pulled off the dirt road before putting it in park. He reached into the satchel on the seat next to him, pulling out a folder and extracting a printed topo map. He opened his car door and got out, squinting to follow the winding dirt road west. Magnus worried that they might be lost. Overhead, a Peregrine falcon flew broad circles high in the air and, catching a thermal, rose effortlessly into the blue sky above the mesa.

"When's the last time you were out this way?" asked Grimes, who'd climbed out of the back seat. His lifted hand shielded his eyes from the bright Colorado sun.

"Been a few years," Pickens admitted, looking down at the map, twisting and turning it in his hand to better orient himself.

Magnus, who'd taken the opportunity to stretch his cramped legs, glowered at Pickens. "Where the hell are we?"

"Twenty-two miles west of Parachute, Colorado, high atop the Grand Mesa, the largest flat mountain in the world," said Pickens. "Our destination isn't far from here."

Magnus eyed the flat plains. Patches of brown sagebrush and the occasional outcropping of blotchy, lichen-covered rock punctuated the mesa's scrub trees and red dirt. To the east, the snowcapped Rockies glistened in the afternoon sun.

"We're not too far from our well sites," Grimes said. Magnus was gratified to hear subservience in the man's tone. *After everything you did ...* "Been a while, but it looks familiar."

Pickens signaled for them to return to the car. Magnus gripped the side handle as they bounced over potholes and ruts. They crested a small rise and headed down the road as it curved past boulders popping out of the dry, gray-green scrub that seemed to cover everything. Pickens slowed the vehicle to a near-crawl, keeping his eyes fixed on the weathered split-rail fence lining the road. Without warning, he stopped, craned his neck in the direction they'd come from, and put the Suburban in reverse. They trundled backward until he spotted what they had come for.

"We're here," Pickens announced. "I think."

Grimes opened the door for Magnus, and they followed Pickens.

"We're crossing under this fence. I want to show you what lies just over there," said Pickens, pointing at a small clearing fifty feet from the fence. Grimes ducked between the split rails to join Pickens on the other side.

Magnus grimaced as he followed, already bemoaning the state of his footwear. Grimes and Pickens kicked up small clouds of dry red dust as they worked their way toward the clearing. Pickens and Grimes were speaking, though Magnus couldn't hear their words. He did hear Grimes whistle with appreciation.

When Magnus caught up, he brushed off his clothes, tidied his hair, and said, "Well? What's so damned impressive?"

"Well, if this doesn't take the cake, I don't know what would," said Grimes, without looking up.

Protruding about a foot out of the red dirt was a cement square about the size of a small dining room table. In the center of the pock-marked slab was an engraved, weathered steel plate.

PROJECT RULISON
NUCLEAR EXPLOSION EMPLACEMENT WELL
Site of the second nuclear gas stimulation experiment in the United States. One 43-kiloton nuclear explosive was detonated in this well, 8,426 feet below the surface on September 10, 1969.

"What does that mean?" Magnus demanded.

"Seems to me," said Grimes, "that these engineers were fracking for gas with atom bombs back in the sixties. I mean, I heard rumors, whispers. Never really thought there could be truth to 'em."

"Not many people know about this," said Pickens. "Back then, it was part of Project Plowshares, the government's attempt to figure out if their new toys—nuclear weapons—could have peaceful applications."

"Imagine that," Grimes said. "A peaceful nuke."

"Between the Rulison explosion in 1969 and the end of Project Plowshares in 1985, the Atomic Energy Commission conducted a total of twenty-seven nuclear tests, detonating thirty-one bombs. Projects with names like Gnome, Vulcan, Marvel, and Gasbuggy were scattered across sites in Alaska, Nevada, New Mexico, Mississippi, and Colorado," said Pickens. "It's something, isn't it?"

Grimes doffed his hat, scrubbed his hand through his hair, and slowly shook his head, as if waiting for the words to sink in. "And you think you can do something similar?"

Pickens grinned. "Oh, I don't think. I know. All I need is the capital."

Grimes turned a startled expression Magnus's way, but Magnus ignored it. Pickens's grin faded.

"Something I should know, gentlemen?" he asked.

"Not a thing," insisted Magnus. "John here's just blown away by the potential." He forced a chuckle. "Get it? Blown away?"

Pickens didn't laugh. Grimes jammed his Stetson back onto his head and tipped it to hide his face in shadows.

"Well, come on then," said Magnus. "Lunch is on me. As long as it comes with an explanation of how we're going to earn more money than we know what to do with, Pickens."

13

There wasn't much to the town of Parachute, Colorado. Located halfway between Grand Junction and Glenwood Springs, they passed a retirement home, school, library, post office, and town hall. Mostly a whole lot of nothing. The sign said it was home to fewer than 1,100 residents.

Their dusty white car wheeled into the gravel drive of the restaurant. The three men walked to a door below a sign that read "Café." Grimes and Pickens ordered cheeseburgers. Magnus ordered a plate of enchiladas, rice, and beans.

"Time's up, Pickens," said Magnus once they'd made decent progress on their meals.

Grimes washed down his last bite of burger with a mouthful of black coffee. "First things first. How did that nuclear fracking business work?"

Pickens finished the last of his shoestring fries and placed his crumpled paper napkin atop his plate. "Imagine digging a shaft a mile and a half deep and detonating a thermonuclear device at the bottom of it." His left hand formed the shape of a downward claw. "You wind up with a large cavern beneath a chimney." He spread his two arms wide, hands extended and pointing at each other. "The cavern created by the blast is so large and unstable that it collapses into itself, breaking apart the rocks and releasing the gas." His arms thrust wide. "Billions of cubic feet of natural gas begin to flow through the chimney."

"Why's this the first we're hearing about it?" asked Grimes.

"The government did their best to keep it under wraps."

"But why?" asked Magnus. "I thought they wanted to get people on board with nukes back then."

"Things didn't entirely go as planned. Following the original Rulison blasts in 1969 and 1970, they flared—burned off—four hundred and thirty million cubic feet of gas into the open sky before capping the well head. Testing showed that levels of radioactivity far exceeded safe standards, and the site was impossible to clean up. Radioactive byproducts of the blast, including tritium, one of the most mobile radiological contaminants known to science, were leaching into the groundwater. The government's plans to use nukes to extract oil and gas from the Green River Formation could potentially have contaminated the groundwater throughout a five-state region, threatening the lives of millions of Americans."

"All right," said Magnus. "So what's changed? Why'd you drag me out here? You're not suggesting we try and use atomic bombs to frack new wells, are you? Last time I checked, the government was pretty stingy with their nukes."

Pickens laughed. "Indeed, Mr. Sawyer. No, sir, that's not what I'm proposing. You see, I've developed another way to do the same thing, only my method is safe and free from radiation."

"Go on," said Grimes, pointing out his empty coffee cup to the lone man working behind the lunch counter.

"I am an engineer and a geologist, not an oilman," said Pickens. "I look at the big picture from a different perspective. Where one might see only problems, I seek out solutions. As I told Mr. Sawyer, the area where your wells are located is part of the richest shale oil and gas deposit on the planet. More than three trillion barrels of oil and gas lie underground in the Green River Valley. The problem's extraction."

Magnus tapped his fingers against the tabletop, urging Pickens to get to the point.

"You've seen the yields we can expect with a thermonuclear device shattering the shale and rocks with its instant heat," said Pickens, wiping his mouth with a paper napkin. "Of course, we can't get our hands on any nukes and, even if we could, we'd never get past today's environmentally sensitive first base."

Magnus twisted his lips in a disapproving scowl before nodding his agreement.

"The Rulison nuclear device yield was rated at forty-three kilotons." Pickens's eyes scanned the two for a sign of their understanding. "That's the same as forty-three thousand tons of TNT." He again scanned their faces and sighed. "All right, look. The problem with a nuke is the radiation. What we need is its explosive force and the heat that's generated. Does that make sense?"

"Go on," said Grimes. "I think I'm following."

"To form the underground cavern and melt the rocks and shale to release the gas when that cavern's ceiling collapses, we need a bomb. But we don't need to split atoms. It could just as easily be TNT."

"Let me get this straight," said Grimes with a dismissive snort. "You're proposing we buy fifty thousand tons of TNT, drop it a mile and a half into the ground, and light the fuse?"

Pickens smiled. "TNT is too expensive and difficult to obtain."

"Get to the point," said Magnus, feeling a small, dangerous prickle of hope beneath his doubt.

"Mining companies blow things up every day. They don't use expensive TNT or dangerous chemicals like nitro anymore. Instead, they use a completely safe material, like ammonia nitrate."

"Fertilizer?" asked Grimes.

"Exactly," said Pickens. "Ammonia nitrate is safe, readily available, and easy to transport. All you do is load up the shot, add just the right amount of fuel oil, and *bam!* You've got yourself the power of a nuclear bomb without the radiation."

"You're pulling my leg, right?" said Magnus.

"No, sir, Mr. Sawyer. No, I am not. We can purchase ammonia nitrate for about five hundred a ton and have it trucked in and loaded down the hole in less than a week. According to my calculations, it'd cost us about twenty million a shot."

Magnus stared at the stick of a man. This was the most outrageous idea he had ever heard ... yet, somehow, it was beginning to make sense. He *wanted* it to make sense. He stiffened in his chair and kept his eyes glued on Pickens.

"So," continued Pickens, "if you do the math, that twenty-million-dollar investment would pay for itself in four or five months of gas production. More importantly, it would continue at that rate for twenty years."

Grimes started peppering Pickens with questions. Pickens pulled a yellow legal pad from his satchel and began sketching out the drilling process. Magnus watched the men's intensity with a detached interest as he ran figures in his head. Fifty million a year per well. One billion over a well's lifespan. At one well per acre—and Empire had thousands of acres under lease—it would mean billions of dollars of revenue. Each well a gold mine. Better than a damned gold mine. They could frack without the environmental hazards, without water, without climate-crazies breathing down their necks. The wells would produce not oil but natural gas: clean, efficient energy for a better world. It could be the salvation of Empire. Hell, perhaps even the entire planet. If the Green River Formation held three trillion barrels of energy just waiting for extraction, the possibilities for his company, for the planet, were endless.

The man behind the counter approached with the bill and all eyes moved toward Magnus. He blinked at the man without recognition, then shook his head as if to clear a fog. He reached into his back pocket for his wallet and extracted a green Amex card.

The trouble was, Empire did not have twenty million dollars to invest in a new well. Empire was days away from collapse. And if Pickens's uneasiness over Grimes's reaction was anything to go by, the man would pick up his plan and run to one of Magnus's competitors the moment he learned how empty the company's coffers were.

As he scrawled his signature on the bottom of the receipt, Magnus knew what he had to do next.

14

Dallas, Texas

Sam wiped his hands on his jeans and checked his watch for what had to be the tenth time in at least as many minutes.

Bowling had seemed a good idea when he first suggested it. There'd be no opportunities for awkward silences, of which there'd been a few since arriving home. So ... conversation, but not too much. If the reviews were right, the bowling alley featured a casual restaurant with tasty food and an impressive cocktail menu.

Now, he wondered. Bowling. *Too cliché?* Given the number of people streaming in, couples as well as larger parties, the place was popular.

Sam was also early. Very early.

And not remotely nervous.

Yeah, right.

The kitschy retro neon sign hummed above him as he tried to radiate nonchalance. Just then his phone buzzed with a text message from Julia; she'd arrived and was trying to find a place to park.

They hadn't talked at all about what happened that night. They probably ought to. They probably would. But not immediately. He *wanted* to talk about it, because it was definitely the sort of thing you discussed after it happened.

How one brought it up, however, was another story entirely.

So, hey, about that survivor's-guilt sex ...

Yeah, no. Not doing that.

Everything else aside, at the end of the day, Sam and Julia didn't know each other that well. There was mutual attraction, yes, but surviving a harrowing life-or-death event wasn't any sort of foundation for a romantic relationship.

Not that Sam had an abundance of excellent role models upon which to make this judgment, but his logic felt sound.

Pushing a hand through his hair, Sam blew out a frustrated breath; the last thing he wanted to think about right now was his father.

Just as he was thinking that maybe he should have partaken of one or two of the impressive cocktails for a hefty dose of liquid courage, Julia walked in, already smiling. She waved as she spotted him, and it struck him how strange it was that he was more accustomed to seeing her in the full-on swaddling of a parka than the jeans and silky top she currently wore. She looked ... good.

Nice, Sam. Real nice. Real smooth. Make sure you say that out loud.

"So," Julia said, raising an inquisitive brow. "Bowling."

"What can I say," Sam replied. "The shoes really do it for me."

When Julia laughed, he could almost forget the way they'd huddled together in Antarctica, half-certain they were about to die as a storm howled around them. "You're a dark horse, aren't you, Sawyer?"

He couldn't quite put his finger on why the sound of his surname on her lips was so pleasing, but he didn't question it.

Her lips curved in an inscrutable smile, and she leaned forward, pressing a kiss to his cheek. Before she pulled away, she whispered, "I should probably warn you ... I take bowling very seriously."

Sam chuckled. "Why doesn't that surprise me?"

"It doesn't?"

"It's possible you have a reputation for being competitive, Bassi."

When Julia let loose a peal of laughter, Sam couldn't pinpoint if the sound was delighted or embarrassed. Maybe a little of both? Either way, he liked that he'd been able to make her laugh.

The bowling alley and restaurant were separated by a cocktail bar, which was already going strong with the happy-hour crowd. Quirky antique bowling memorabilia graced the walls.

The cocktail menu was an impressive collection of classics and some newer recipes developed by the bar staff.

"You know, I've always wanted to try a Sazerac," Julia said.

"Gotta respect the old-school cocktails."

"What about you?"

Sam considered. "Their Old Fashioned looks good."

"That one caught my eye, too. I can't hate anything that uses a craft whiskey."

Once their cocktails had arrived, food was ordered, and bowling shoes donned, one of the awkward silences Sam had been hoping to avoid fell. Sam raised his glass. "Here's to not freezing to death at the end of the world?"

Julia chuckled as she clinked the edge of her glass to his. "Didn't we already celebrate that in Mexico?"

Sam flushed, and it had nothing to do with the potency of his drink. "I wasn't sure if we were going to, uh, jump right into—"

"Bed?" Julia interjected, grinning as Sam sputtered. "Look, we're both grown-ups. Granted, I usually know a guy's favorite color, favorite meal, and, like, birthday before we sleep together, but ... " She shrugged. "I don't regret it. Do you?"

Sam opened his mouth, closed it again, took another sip of his drink, and then shook his head. "I ... really don't. At all."

This time when Julia leaned in for a kiss, she didn't press her lips to his cheek.

As dates went, this one was already ranking high on Julia's list of all-time favorites. Drinking good drinks and absolutely walloping someone at something competitive were both favorite pastimes. And the fact that Sam wasn't pouting or posturing about the loss boded well.

The kissing wasn't bad, either. In fact, the kissing was damn near perfect.

They tumbled out of the Uber outside his apartment building, still holding hands and giddy with laughter and the kisses they'd refrained from indulging in to preserve Sam's star rating. Julia was about to rectify this situation when she realized they had an audience. A pair of grim-faced men stood outside the building. She'd have bet tenure that they were plain-clothed cops.

The laughter froze in her throat. Whatever Sam saw in her expression made him turn, half-shielding her.

"Can I help you?" Sam asked.

"Sam Sawyer?"

For a moment, Julia was back in Antarctica as Uzziel and his goons rounded them up like cattle. She half-expected the bearded madman to emerge from the shadows and start proselytizing. She cast a glance around them, but they were alone on the street. Even the Uber had disappeared.

"Can I help you?" Sam repeated with a touch more steel.

The taller of the two men stepped forward and became markedly less grim-faced. Julia mentally dubbed him Good Cop and the other one Bad Cop.

Good Cop flashed his ID and, to his credit, let them both look at it long enough to deem it authentic. "Mr. Sawyer, I'm Detective—"

"Doctor Sawyer," Julia corrected before mentally slapping a hand over her eyes. That last cocktail had clearly contained some distilled stupidity in lieu of Dutch courage.

Detective Good Cop stopped, cleared his throat, and began again. "Dr. Sawyer, I'm Detective Campbell and this is Detective Matthews. We have been sent to collect you over a matter of some importance."

"Collect me?" Sam echoed. "What's the important matter?"

"You are a person of interest in a fraud complaint, and we would like to ask you some questions."

Sam tensed as Julia's stomach fell somewhere to the vicinity of her shoes. Fraud. Like the perhaps-somewhat-illicit means through which a certain journey to Antarctica was funded. *Son of a bitch.*

"Are you arresting me, Detective Campbell?" Sam asked.

"No," Campbell said, shaking his head. "There are just some questions that need answers."

"Call a lawyer," Julia hissed in Sam's ear. "Don't say a damn thing to any of them without a lawyer."

His nod was almost imperceptible.

"Apologies to the young woman," Campbell said. "But you'll need to come along with us."

A muscle jumped in Sam's jaw. "I'll go with you as soon as things here are settled." He paused, inclining his head. "Unless you're afraid I'm going to skip town in the next ten minutes?"

Campbell nodded at his partner. "We'll be in the car. When you're ready."

Once the cops had retreated to their unmarked patrol car, Sam turned to Julia and pressed his keys into her hand. "Go inside. Take however long you need to sober up. Let Harry know what happened. This might blow over, it might not."

"Sam, you can't just—"

He turned to face her, his jaw set. "Grimes and I used Empire's funds without permission," he said, his voice low and tense. "That chicken just came home to roost sooner than expected. I can't let him twist in the wind when he put his ass on the line for us. For Satsky."

"Then let me come with you. I can—"

Sam pushed a hand through his hair, already shaking his head. "The less you're involved, the better. I really don't want you to get pulled into whatever power play my dad's got going here." Gently, he touched his fingertips to her cheekbone. "Besides, someone's got to take care of Sky."

Julia pulled her bottom lip between her teeth and swallowed the protest begging to be released. The shift in Sam's expression when he said the words "my dad" and "Grimes" made her pause.

Whatever else happened, she didn't want to add to the burden of his worries.

She rose on her toes and pressed a swift kiss to his lips, if only to see that haunted look of his shift into a smile. Then, she watched him get into the car. Watched him close the door. Watched him drive off.

He didn't look back. She couldn't look away.

And the keys dangling from her numb fingers weighed a thousand pounds.

15

Dallas, Texas, Twenty Years Ago:

Texas summers were brutal. But the heat outside was nothing compared to the fire burning up Sam's spine, clear to the tips of his ears.

He was about to be found out. He knew it.

Sam had tried for a full twelve and a half years to try and gain his father's approval. Tried and failed, his entire life. It didn't matter what he attempted, the result was always the same: Sam, fumbling around to find something he could do to make Magnus proud, and then falling flat on his face in the process.

This year, he promised himself, it'd be different. This year he started seventh grade. This year there'd be football.

He didn't want to ask permission to play; that would just end with his father saying or doing something that left Sam feeling like he had no business making the effort. Mr. Grimes would fix it for him. He always did.

Grimes drove Sam to tryouts in his pickup truck. They rode in companionable silence until Grimes cleared his throat and broke it.

"You sure this is a good idea, Sam?"

Sam shrugged one shoulder. "It's just tryouts. If I don't make it, nothing'll change."

"And if you do?" Grimes asked. "What then?"

Sam chewed the inside of his lip. "Maybe he'll be happy about it." Maybe he'll be happy about me, for once.

"Listen here, kid. You can do all sorts of things to try and get a reaction out of your dad. Hell, he's lucky you ain't breaking windows and spray-painting bridges to get a rise out of him. But some things . . . some things you gotta do for yourself, and to hell with the old man."

"Like this?"

Grimes nodded. "If you make that team, you're gonna to be part of it whether or not your dad's happy. If he's pissed off, you're still on the team. They'll be counting on you. You better make sure you can live with the results, even if you don't get what you want out of the experiment."

Sam traced the lines in the seat leather with a fingertip. "So . . . make sure I want it before I try?"

"Bingo."

Tryouts came, tryouts went. It was the most grueling week of Sam's life, filled with more drills and assessments than he ever could have imagined. More than once, he wanted to walk away from it all. Some kids did. He learned the rules, learned what was expected of him—Sam applied the same energy to learning the game as he applied to his academic subjects.

By the end of it all, he made the junior-high team; he was officially the second-string running back.

When it came time to deliver the news, Sam approached his father in his study after dinner. Mr. Grimes was there, and the two were going over some blueprints.

"Sir?"

Magnus glanced up then back at the document spread across his desk. "What is it?"

Sam looked quickly at Grimes, then back at his father. He delivered his news, unsure of what to expect. With his hands clasped behind his back, he crossed his fingers for luck.

Whatever Sam expected, it wasn't what he got. Magnus just stared at him.

No. Through him.

"You?" Magnus said, incredulity dripping from that single syllable. "They put you on a football team? You're what, ninety pounds soaking wet?"

"Yes, sir," he replied, somehow managing not to stammer. "Running back. Second-string."

His father looked him up and down and snorted. "Second-string. Figures."

Grimes, though, chuckled and reached over to muss Sam's hair with one huge hand. "Come on now, boss. That's the best place for him to learn. Nothing to be ashamed of. We don't throw the greenhorns to the wolves out in the fields, either. We'd scare 'em off."

Magnus scoffed, as if to say that maybe they'd be better off scaring some folks into a new job. Sam waited for him to say something else—anything else—but his father only lifted a hand to shoo him away as he returned his attention to the papers spread out before him.

Magnus didn't show up to a single game that year. He didn't even go to any game Sam played in once he made the team again in eighth grade and was promoted to first-string.

John Grimes came, though. To every single game.

After a while, familiar faces from Empire turned up in the stands. Just never Magnus's.

When Sam made the high school team, all his father said was, "Of course you did. It's just a 3A school."

Even when Sam worked his way through the ranks and made the high school varsity team, Magnus remained unimpressed. When Sam studied his ass off and won the school's Student Athlete of the Year award in his sophomore, junior, and senior years, John Grimes attended the awards banquet.

Sam was pretty sure everyone at school thought Grimes was his father.

Hell, sometimes he wished it was the truth.

In Sam's senior year, the team reached the district playoffs. They'd always come close to going to the state championships, but this year they had an actual chance. A good one.

"So, you win, and the team goes to State," Magnus said, sitting in the big leather chair in his office.

Sam nodded. "That's right."

Magnus leaned back in his chair, leather creaking, and laced his hands behind his head. "All right," he said. "You convinced me. I'll go."

"Go?" Sam echoed.

"To the game."

In that moment, something that hadn't occurred to Sam in the last six years of his educational career became abruptly and painfully clear—he hadn't wanted Magnus at any of his games. And he especially didn't want him at this one. He also realized Magnus was watching him, very obviously expecting a thank you.

"Oh." Swallowing hard, he added, "Great. That's great."

It wasn't convincing, but Magnus didn't seem to notice.

The game went into overtime; spirits were high despite the even match between them and the other team. They were moving the ball, putting points on the board. Sam carried the ball into the end-zone several times that night, and he was on his way again when a defensive tackle nailed him out of nowhere, stripping the ball from his arms. The referees called it a fumble.

The first, last, and only game Magnus attended, and it was a loss.

Once they were home, Sam went outside while his father fumed indoors, muttering about all the things he could have been doing with his very valuable time instead of watching his son literally drop the ball and destroy his team's chance at State.

Sam sat on the porch swing and listened to the cicadas. After a while, his phone buzzed with a text message. From Grimes.

You doing okay?

He almost didn't respond, largely because he wasn't sure how to answer the question. Been better, he typed.

I bet. Has the boss stopped bellyaching yet?

What do you think?

Didn't turn out how we'd like, but it was still a damn good game. You've come a long way. Nothing to be ashamed of.

With one leg, Sam gave the porch swing a push and slowly tapped out his reply:

Nope. And I think I got what I wanted out of the experiment either way.

16

Dallas, Texas

Even tipsy from the drinks he'd shared with Julia, it didn't take Sam long to realize that the cops weren't taking him to the nearest station. Instead, they followed the irritatingly familiar route from Sam's condo complex to the house in which he'd grown up.

"Seriously?" he said, leaning forward. "My dad put you up to this?"

Neither of the cops so much as looked at him.

"Look, if it's all the same to you, I'd like you to turn around and take me home," Sam said. "I'm not interested in playing my dad's little games."

Campbell turned his head, his expression stern. "Dr. Sawyer, we're doing you a courtesy, here. Your father called in a favor, yes. It's one you should be grateful for."

Sam snorted and slumped against the rear seat. "Spoken like someone who doesn't know Magnus Sawyer particularly well."

Campbell raised an eyebrow. "Spoken like someone looking to add a felony or two to his pristine rap sheet."

"Are you threatening me?"

Campbell shook his head and sighed. "No, kid. I'm really not. Based on what your dad says, you dug this grave all by yourself. I think he's trying to give you an honest out."

"Honest and Magnus Sawyer don't belong in the same sentence," Sam muttered.

"So you didn't max out the company card you weren't supposed to have, steal a bunch of equipment from said company, and flee the country with a few of said company's employees?"

Though the alcohol in his system begged him to defend himself, protest, explain why he'd made the choices he'd made, Sam wisely held his tongue.

"Yeah, thought so," said Campbell. "Just hear your dad out. Pretty sure we can still cart you off to jail afterward, if that's what you really want."

The urge to roll his eyes like a petulant teenager was strong, but Sam resisted it by remembering that Grimes had gone back to Empire first—and that Grimes didn't deserve whatever punishment Magnus was undoubtedly cooking up for him.

By the time they turned into the drive of the Sawyer mansion, Sam had sobered up just enough to recognize the multiple sedimentary levels of shit in which he found himself. When he glanced at his phone, he noted that it was nearly midnight, his battery was at five percent, and he'd missed half a dozen calls and text messages, all from Julia. He scanned through the texts, but when he tried to call into his voicemail, his battery gave up the ghost before the first message could start playing.

Sam half-expected the cops to cuff him or drag him inside by the earlobe or something equally humiliating. If he knew Magnus, it was what he'd want. A reason to feel big, tough, powerful. When it came to dick-swinging competitions, his dad had no equal. But Campbell only opened the rear door of the car and gestured Sam toward the house.

"Don't run," Campbell said. "I'm tired, but you're still drunk. And neither of us wants to add resisting arrest as the cherry on this shit sundae."

Under different circumstances, Sam thought he and Detective Campbell might even have been friends. So, instead of pouting —*serious scientists do not pout*—he only straightened his shoulders and headed toward the front door.

He'd always known he'd have to pay the piper, after all. He just hadn't expected the invoice to come in quite so soon.

17

Pickens had wanted to move quickly. Hell, so did Magnus. The sooner they started work, the sooner he could get all the money-grubbing debt collectors off his back.

When he had talked to Havens, his CFO, the man outright laughed in his face. "You've got to be kidding, Magnus. I'd struggle to scrounge up twenty bucks, right now. Twenty million? No chance. And no bank in the world is going to back this horse. The glue truck is on its way." Havens shook his head. "Maybe if you got Sam to come—"

"Leave him out of it," Magnus had snarled. "That ingrate's the last person I—" Magnus fell abruptly silent as Havens lifted an eyebrow.

"You sure about that? The contingency Henry put—"

Magnus silenced the man with the cut of his hand, but Havens's smile only widened.

"How much?" Magnus had asked.

"Enough," replied Havens. "More than enough, after all this time. But there's no two ways about it. You gotta get your kid back on Board. And we both know that when God was handing out stubbornness, he gave Sam twice his share."

But the wheels were already turning. "You leave that part to me."

Despite the certainty with which he'd spoken to Havens, Magnus scanned the papers spread over his desk for the fifth time in an hour, searching in vain for a way to circumvent the various restrictions standing between him and the magnitude of wealth represented by the Green River Formation opportunity. None miraculously appeared. He wondered if God had tempted Job the same way—shown him paradise never before imagined, only to snatch it away again on a technicality.

Not this time. Not tonight.

By the time Sam walked in, looking disheveled and irritated—not that Magnus expected anything different—Magnus was already sitting behind the impenetrable fortress of his desk. Henry Sawyer scowled down at them both from the portrait on the wall.

Not this time, old man, Magnus thought. *This time I take, and you lose.*

Magnanimously, Magnus waved to the chair opposite his desk. Sam rolled his eyes and remained standing.

"You've made your point, Dad," Sam said. "Can we skip to the punchline?"

Rage bubbled up hot and instant, like a geyser blowing its top. Magnus couldn't hide the grimace as he wrestled it down again. With a tight smile, he said, "If that's what you want, son. You start tomorrow."

Sam glanced skyward, as if praying to the God Magnus doubted his son even believed in. "I have a job, Dad. Salaried and everything. Great healthcare plan."

"You're in no position to make jokes," Magnus said through gritted teeth.

Sam sighed. "Or what? You'll have your pet cops arrest me? What kind of favor did the department owe you, anyway?"

"You have never understood the importance of making friends in high places."

"Don't you mean *buying* friends in high places?"

Magnus brought the flat of his hand down on his desk hard enough to make the papers jump. A little of the smugness drained from his son's expression. "You owe me. And this is how you'll repay that debt."

"Dad—"

"Or John Grimes will pay it. You have any idea what kind of sentence First-degree felony theft comes with? He'll lose every goddamned thing he's ever owned, and he'll die behind bars."

Sam stumbled as he sank into the chair. The smugness was entirely gone, now, replaced by the lily-livered cowardice Magnus knew all too well. "You wouldn't do that. He's—he's been your man for over forty years—"

"Apparently not," Magnus said. "Apparently, he's been yours."

"I needed—you don't understand—a friend was in danger—"

Magnus leaned back in his chair and folded his arms over his chest. "And your harebrained scheme got two of my best men killed. Doesn't seem like a fair trade. Especially since John tells me there's no recovering even a single piece of that equipment. Did you honestly think you wouldn't face consequences for your actions?" He shook his head. "I don't know where I went wrong with you."

Sam seemed to shrink, to shrivel like a leaf caught surprised by the arrival of autumn. Magnus nearly laughed. After all this time, all these struggles, all the sheer embarrassment of having *this* disappointment of a child to carry on the family legacy, it brought him no end of comfort to see him finally humbled.

"Grimes isn't to blame," Sam said in the quiet voice of a near-broken man. "If you're going to punish anyone, punish me."

Magnus half-rose from his chair and leaned over the desk. "I *am.*"

When Sam lifted his chin, a ghost of his old defiance still haunted his eyes. "Why are you like this?"

"I could ask you the same question," Magnus replied, "but I already know the answer. I was too easy on you. Let weaklings like John Grimes raise you. Let women tell me what was best for my own son. You're weak, Samuel Sawyer. You're weak, and this is the only way I can make you strong."

"Why does my working or not working for Empire matter to you?" Sam's tone was nearly plaintive now; it made Magnus's stomach turn. "If I'm as weak as you say, why would you want me associated with you or this place?"

"We're blood," snapped Magnus. "You're not the son I'd have asked for, but you're still blood. Empire's your legacy. Blood sticks together." Magnus tapped a finger against one of the folders on his desk. "But don't go getting any ideas. This here's a report from my private detective. In it, he lists every goddamned person who has so much as looked sideways at you since you and Grimes went on your little crime spree. You fail me, you turn on me, you run away, you have *any contact whatsoever* with anyone from your old life, and I bring down hell by way of charges. You. John Grimes. That pretty little thing you've been tooling around with. The old professor. Every *damned one is an accessory,* Samuel. That part of your life is over. Or the rest of their lives will be spent behind bars. You understand me?"

Sam dropped his face into his hands. Magnus watched the boy's shoulders tremble. *Weak.* "How long?" Sam asked, words muffled.

"As long as it takes," Magnus said. "And without a single goddamned word of complaint. Understood?"

Sam lifted his head and nodded.

"What's that, boy?" Magnus demanded.

"Yes, sir," Sam said, finally cowed. Finally humbled. Finally exactly where Magnus had always wanted him. "Understood."

18

Dallas, Texas

When the phone rang early the next morning, Julia answered without even looking at the caller. "Sam?"

"'Fraid not," came the familiar but unexpected voice of John Grimes. "Did I wake you?"

"I didn't sleep," said Julia. "I was waiting—where's Sam? What's going on?"

"I, uh, y'see—"

"Don't pull that Texas cowboy nonsense with me, John. What happened to Sam?"

"Sam wanted me—that is, I—there's no easy way to explain this, Julia. Sam's gone back to Empire."

"Gone ... back? What do you mean?"

"Well, his daddy made him an offer he couldn't refuse. That's how he explained it to me. But, uh, it came with strings."

"Strings," Julia repeated. At her feet, Sky tilted his head and uttered a low, questioning whine.

"No contact with anyone from his, well—no contact with any of you."

Julia couldn't help it. She laughed. "I'm sorry, *what?* Last I checked, Sam was a grown man. He's not a teenager who broke curfew."

Grimes sighed heavily. "I know how it sounds."

The hysterical laughter just wouldn't *stop.* Sky put a paw on her knee, and Julia reached down to bury a hand in his ruff. Something real. Something tangible.

"But there's more," Grimes said. "And you ain't gonna like it any better than you've liked any part of this conversation so far."

"Of course there's more," Julia said. Her eyes stung with unshed tears. "Go on. It can't get weirder."

"Sam thinks you should, uh, lie low for a bit. Real low. Out of sight low."

"You realize this sounds insane."

Grimes cleared his throat. "Julia, this is bigger than either of us, you understand? The kinda money that gets thrown around, well, it buys things most people wouldn't think of buying. Hell, that most people wouldn't realize can be bought. His dad's got something up his —well. If Sam's worried, I'm worried, is all I'm saying. And the doc did say you could stay there at the IFDC, didn't she?"

Julia pinched the bridge of her nose, but it wasn't enough to clear her mind after the sleepless night. "If this is some kind of joke ... "

Grimes said, "Ma'am, I don't think anyone's been joking since a severed ear showed up in the mail."

Julia uttered a few choice expletives under her breath. Sky replaced the paw on her leg with his chin.

"Fine," she said. "I'll go to the IFDC. You tell Sam that if he decides to grow up and live his own life, maybe he can give me a call. Gotta tell you, though, John. Right now? I'm not sure I'll answer."

"I'll keep you in the loop."

Julia scoffed and hung up the phone. She grabbed her laptop and emailed Harry about moving in to the IFDC dorms. Then she buried her face in Sky's warm fur. "Well, buddy, looks like it's just you and me. How do you feel about living in a mall for a while?"

Sky's tail thumped against the hardwood floor.

"I can pack for a six-week trip in a backpack and a single piece of carry-on luggage."

Sky made a noise deep in his throat. To Julia's ears, it sounded incredulous.

"Okay, fine, four weeks. My point is, you have your own suitcase. It's not small. And it's full."

His tail thumped again.

"Yes, I know. I'm the one who packed your bag. I thought I was just bringing essentials."

Sky pushed to his feet and left the room. He came back momentarily with a stuffed alligator in his mouth. He squeaked the toy once and dropped it.

"No."

Sky cocked his head and let out a low groan.

"I said no."

That low groan went up in pitch.

"There's no room, Sky," she argued.

Sky picked up the toy again. He squeaked it once, firmly.

Seconds ticked by. The absurdity of it all was too much, and Julia finally laughed. "Okay, fine, Harpo. Fine. You win this round. Alligator comes along."

Sky hopped on the couch with the toy and began squeaking it joyfully. And maybe a little victoriously. Shaking her head, she picked up her half-drained coffee cup. It was warm but not hot, so she downed it and washed the mug quickly in the kitchen sink before pouring what remained in the carafe into the insulated travel mug that had been nearly as many places as Julia had. Her lucky mug.

"Okay. Necessities, check."

Sky squeaked the toy again.

"Dog food, bowls, treats, bacon-flavored chew-bones, check." Julia carefully avoided thinking about why she had to make a late-night run to the pet store for dog supplies.

Sky squeaked the gator again, yanking her attention back to the moment.

"Bloody annoying squeaky toy, check."

She checked the locks on all the windows and doors in her townhouse, then double-checked the automatic security timer to dim her lights and turn them on again. She tucked the travel mug into a side pocket on her backpack and plucked the living room curtain away to peek out the front window. In the pre-dawn gloom, a dark SUV pulled into the driveway. Illuminated only by headlights, the driver rolled down the window and gave a brief wave.

They slipped out of the front door into the predawn darkness where the IFDC driver was waiting. Sky stiffened at the sight of the vehicle, then as Julia opened the rear door, he entered first, sniffing around the seats and finally settling down with a satisfied grunt. The driver, a silent figure in the pre-dawn darkness, merely nodded and drove off.

The streets were quiet; Dallas at large hadn't yet woken. Aside from a few cars, likely belonging to students heading early to campus or shift-workers heading either to work or back home again, traffic was practically nonexistent.

The driver broke the silence first. "It's all kinda cloak and dagger, isn't it?"

Julia chuckled. "A little, yeah."

"I'm Shannon, by the way."

"Julia."

Shannon laughed. "Oh, believe me. Your name? I know."

"Should I be flattered or worried?"

"Flattered. Totally flattered. I'm one of Doc Bickford's strays. She usually sticks to working with the graduate students, but I made enough of a pest of myself that she took me on as an independent study."

"How'd you get involved with all this?"

"Don't know that I'd say I'm involved. Mostly I'm a general dogsbody. I do the grocery shopping, I handle pick-ups and drop-offs, run whatever errands need running, that sort of thing."

Julia looked out the window, absorbing the sights, while Sky's nose pressed against the glass on the opposite side of the car, his breath fogging it up. Buildings loomed like giants, their windows darkened, while streetlamps cast pools of yellow light on the layer of dew on the road. The occasional homeless person wrapped in tattered blankets, a stray cat darting across the road, and the distant wail of a siren were their only companions.

The car wound through the empty city streets, passing tall buildings that loomed like silent sentinels. Elegant storefronts gave way to warehouses and deserted factories. Graffiti adorned the walls.

The first time she and Sam had come to IFDC headquarters, they'd gone in the front door, so to speak. But Shannon was driving to the opposite end of the sprawling structure. She navigated the desolate parking lot, following a pattern of faded painted arrows that led them down a shallow tunnel, and further down to a pitch-dark underground parking garage. The blackness was eased only by the SUV's headlights.

"How can you—" Julia began, but Shannon waved a hand, cutting her off.

"It takes a second for the motion sensors—"

Suddenly the cavernous parking area was lit with flickering fluorescent lights. Julia blinked at the sudden brightness.

"—to pick up a vehicle," Shannon finished. "They only stay on for about five minutes, so we'll want to get a move on unloading you."

Julia shouldered her backpack and snapped up the handle of her rolling carry-all before taking Sky's leash. The dog jumped out as effortlessly as he jumped in and gave a shake. Shannon hefted Sky's suitcase from the back of the SUV, grunting with effort.

"Kibble," Julia supplied, apologetically.

"Hey, every member of the team's gotta eat, right?"

Sky gave a sharp bark.

About ten feet from the door, Shannon's watch chirped. A tinny male voice with a British accent came from the vicinity of her wrist. "Oi, Bernard, lights out in five ... four ... "

Shannon broke into a jog. Julia followed; Sky took the hint and ran alongside her.

"Three ... two ... one."

The parking garage plunged into sudden darkness that lasted for barely a second before a metallic ka-chunk echoed through the space. Light spilled out, pushing back the blackness and casting a glow around Shannon's mad curls.

She grinned over her shoulder at Julia. "We try to look out for each other around here."

Another chirp came from her wrist, followed by the same tinny voice. "I'm not hearing a thank you."

Making a face, Shannon let the door close after Julia, and pressed down a button on her watch. "Thank you, Reginald."

Shannon led Julia to the dorms where she and Sky would be hanging their hats for the foreseeable future. If nothing else, Julia was grateful for the help with her luggage. Shannon pulled Sky's suitcase behind her easily as they chatted. Relieved of his leash, Sky trotted contently between them.

The dormitories were comfortable, if spartan in decor. Julia sat on the twin bed and gave an experimental bounce before nodding her approval. Whoever chose the amenities knew the importance of a good night's sleep, at least.

"If there's anything else you need, I can either run and get it from your place or you can put in a requisition for it," Shannon said.

Shannon left with a promise to drop by later and with a blanket offer to walk Sky any time of day or night. Shortly after she left, there came a knock at the door and Julia opened it expecting to find Shannon on the other side; when she saw Harry, Julia did a double take.

"I ran into Shannon a couple of minutes ago. She said you were getting settled in."

Julia stepped aside, inviting Harry in. "There's not a whole lot to settle as of yet, but I'm just about unpacked. Something on your mind?"

"There always is. Any word from Sam yet?"

Julia shook her head. “Not yet. I don’t have a good feeling about any of it. The officers he left with said he wasn’t being arrested, but Sam seemed to think the whole thing was his father’s doing.” She shrugged. “I’m not sure where that leaves him ... or the rest of us.”

“He’ll check in. I saw it in his face the other day—that boy is champing at the bit to get elbow deep into all this. His daddy may deter Sam, might even delay him, but I’ll be damned surprised if the devil himself could dissuade him.”

“I hope you’re right.” Julia folded her arms and surveyed the little dorm. After a moment, she sighed. “Harry. I have to ask. Just one question.”

“Just the one? I’m impressed.”

Julia turned to face Harry. “You have computer savants, mapmakers, language geniuses, fusion experts—even a code-breaker, for Pete’s sake. I don’t know the first thing about fusion technology, Harry. Sam doesn’t either. I know I’m flattered to be included, but I’m not entirely sure what either of us bring to the project, given our respective fields. We’re scientists, yes. But physicists? No.”

“Because your expertise comes down to patterns in the climate, rather than building the technology to address and potentially correct those patterns?”

Julia let out a long breath. “Yes. None of what you’re trying to accomplish here depends on identifying the problems we’re trying to solve. Hell, the problems have damn near been identified by this point.”

Harry crossed the room and sat down on a small sofa. Sky immediately hopped up next to her and shoved his head under her hand. Absently, she started petting him.

“I could say that it’s just a matter of being in the wrong place at the wrong time. Or the right place at the right time. All depends on how you look at it. Your leadership skills were gained through field experience and your introduction to Eemian technology give you a leg up over most people, but I suspect that’s not the answer you’re looking for.”

Julia gave a helpless shrug. "I can't get to work until I know what the work is. What my job is. What my place is here."

"And I can't blame you for asking. Obviously, you need clear parameters and an understanding of what's expected of you."

"Yes. Please."

Harry fell silent for several seconds, her hand never straying from Sky's head. "Here's what I know. I know that the IFDC have already solved one of the largest problems involved in building a fusion reactor: starting and containing the fusion reaction. Problem is, we have no practical method of delivering the fuel to keep it going. Karl believed—and I agree—that the Eemians knew how to convert gaseous hydrogen into a stable metal."

"Which they then used for fuel," Julia finished for her.

"Yes," Harry said.

"But—"

Julia looked away. "I want to help, Harry. But I don't see how I can. What do you need from a climate scientist?"

Harry's eyes twinkled as she leaned in, her voice dropping to a whisper. "The Eemians, Julia. We need their secrets."

"Sorry, Harry, but the Eemians...they're gone. Uzziel and his thugs melted all the evidence. I don't see how....

Harry smiled and put her hand up for silence.

"I know, child, I know. Believe me.

"Look, Julia, I understand your field of study is climate. Neither of us is a physicist or has anything to offer the scientists and engineers at the IFDC when it comes to advancing the completion of a working fusion reactor."

Julia nodded.

"But, here's the thing. Without civilization's ability to generate power and not add to the planet's carbon load, we're going to see a repeat of what happened to the Eemians."

Julia's brows furrowed and she reached down to scratch Sky's ears so she wouldn't have to meet the pain in Harry's eyes.

"I don't need to remind you that the Eemian civilization met the same fate we are headed towards," Harry said. "They too generated a climate disaster by spewing billions of tons of carbon into the air to create power. Look at the consequences: all of Greenland melted, half of Antarctica, most of the North Pole — gone. The seas rose nearly 100 feet. Those Eemians known as Sahu, who refused to acknowledge the danger, either perished or were forced back to their starting point, struggling in caves for the next 90,000 years."

Julia nodded. "But why work on something so technologically challenging as fusion? There's plenty of alternative energy solutions..."

"Sure," said Harry. "But solar works only when the sun shines, and wind is converted to electrical power only when it is blowing. Our civilization consumes about 174,000 Terawatts of energy a year. All the alternative energy solutions combined produce only about 1.5% of that number. No, to stop the climate crisis we need to replace 100% of the energy needs with a zero carbon solution. And do it quickly. Fusion. The Eemians had it figured out."

“Sad,” said Julia, “that all we have left from the Eemians is that artifact and a few photos.”

Harry's eyes twinkled. "Not exactly, Julia.” She slid a folder full of photos across the worn table. "Take a look at these." Her soft voice was a blend of excitement and assurance.

Julia's hands trembled as she recognized the photos Sam had taken from inside the Eemian pyramid. Harry pulled out one in particular and handed Julia a magnification loupe. "Look closely at that small section of the photo."

Julia's eyes narrowed as she inspected the image. "It looks like maybe it's some sort of drawing or map."

"Right! We believe it is a map to the other Eemian Sanctuaries.

"Remember back to Greenland and that small sanctuary you and Karl uncovered? We believe it is one of several scattered around the world. We suspect that map in the photograph will identify the locations of all the sanctuaries, but we've not yet figured out how to read it. Your challenge, if you're up for it, will be to lead the team to figure out how to read the map and then travel wherever it takes you to uncover the Eemian secrets and help us save the planet from climate collapse."

"I don't know anything about deciphering maps or leading teams on missions," she protested. "And saving the planet from climate collapse? Me? I am just a researcher."

Harry's gaze was unwavering. "You're more than that, Julia. You've been on some wild adventures in Greenland and Antarctica already, and there's no one more qualified and brave. Besides, Sky will lead the way." A hint of humor danced in her eyes.

A moment of silence settled over the room as Julia mulled over Harry's words. The task was immense, the stakes even higher. She glanced down at Sky, who wagged his tail, as if encouraging her to take the challenge.

"But how will we even begin?" Julia asked.

Harry's smile was gentle and reassuring. "With the combined knowledge of the IFDC team and the resources we have, we can figure it out. You won't be alone, Julia. We're all in this together."

Julia's eyes flickered with uncertainty. The proposition was staggering. The risks, the unknowns, the magnitude of the responsibility. It all weighed heavily on her.

"But Harry, this is unlike anything I've ever done before," she stammered. "Deciphering ancient maps? Leading a global expedition? What if I fail? What if I lead us down the wrong path?"

Harry leaned forward, her gaze steady and her voice calm. "Julia, think back to all the obstacles you've already overcome. The dangers you've faced, the discoveries you've made. You've proven time and again that you have the courage, the intellect, and the resilience to tackle the unknown."

Julia shook her head, her doubts clawing at her. "But this is different, Harry. Those were field studies, scientific research. This is a quest, a mission that could change the course of human history. And what if we're wrong about the map? What if it's not a map at all?"

Harry reached across the table, gripping Julia's hands. "I believe in you, and I believe in what we've found. I've seen you in action, Julia. You have a way of seeing things others don't. You have an intuition that goes beyond the logical mind. That's why you're the right person for this mission."

Julia looked into Harry's eyes, searching for the certainty she didn't feel.

"Take your time," Harry said softly, sensing Julia's turmoil. "Think it over. Talk to Sky," she added with a gentle smile, nodding towards the husky.

A silence settled over the room as Julia's thoughts swirled. She looked down at Sky, who seemed to sense her struggle, his eyes meeting hers with a canine wisdom. For a moment it seemed as if he were nodding his head. Impossible. She thought about the sanctuaries, the hidden knowledge of the Eemians, the potential to alter the future of humanity. Her fears were real, but so was the opportunity. She thought about Sam and the possibility of their futures together. She thought about her father and how he would have encouraged her to go for it. He always did.

"I'll do it," she finally said, her voice stronger now. "I'll lead the mission. I'll make it happen."

19

Dallas, Texas

Julia found something about the linguistics area innately appealing. Welcoming. Harry had called the group analog, and while there were more ink and paper books in this section than there were elsewhere in the whole IFDC complex, she spotted reassuring touches of modernity as well: at each research table was an interactive projection screen displaying different bits and snatches of what had been collected so far of the Quondan language. At each station, researchers worked intently. Someone swore every now and then, temporarily breaking the silence that then settled back into place like thick snowfall.

Dr. Faulkner sat at one long wooden table, a laptop in front of her and an electronic tablet at her elbow. Photographs depicting examples of the Quondan language were placed carefully in front of her, each with different notes written in white pencil. Her curls were in wild disarray, as if she'd been running frustrated fingers through her hair all morning. Though she'd been dressed casually the day before, today Julia found her in blue jeans and a Harvard sweatshirt.

"Dr. Faulkner?"

She put up one finger, the universal signal for wait, please. A moment or two later she looked up. "Ah! Dr. Bassi. I was wondering when we'd meet."

"Please, call me Julia." She grinned.

"Please, call me Betty. Elizabeth, if you must."

"Harry thought I should drop by and begin attempting to get a grasp on my Quondan."

Betty stifled a laugh. "What do you know about dead languages, Julia?"

"Whatever I learned was while I was an undergrad."

"Which probably wasn't much and has almost certainly been supplanted by something else of more use to you," she replied archly.

Julia chuckled. "Most likely."

"In that case, I'll give you the Reader's Digest version of what we're attempting here," Betty said, speaking as briskly as she had in yesterday's meeting. "When scholars started decoding cuneiform, they had to basically reverse engineer the language using, among other things, writing on ancient Persian monuments. If one monument said, 'Dedicated to Ted, A Most Excellent Farmer,' let's just say, scholars could extrapolate a name, a superlative, an adjective, and a noun. Doesn't seem like much, but if you study enough monuments, you collect more and more names, adjectives, and common nouns." Betty smiled. "I know that look. You see the problem already."

"A shortage of Quondan monuments, for one."

"Bingo. And since cuneiform influenced later languages, scholars could—over years, mind you, decades—slowly piece together hints and clues that helped them decode cuneiform. Good news is, the samples of Quondan writing that we do have seem to bear a resemblance to proto-cuneiform. Bad news is, we don't have a whole lot of samples. There's more good news, though. And bad news. Lots of both, so I won't bore you with the 'which do you want first' rigmarole." Betty moved to a clear section of the table and sat upon one corner. Julia followed her cue and pulled over a chair.

"Basically," Betty continued, "languages follow the paths of the people who spoke them. Our tribe of Quondans who left Antarctica very likely eventually wound up in or around ancient Babylon. Their writing influenced the cuneiform languages," she said, indicating to a heavily marked photo of Quondan writing. "See? That's a little too close to cuneiform to be coincidence."

"Do you mean to tell me," Julia said slowly, "this is basically ... proto-proto-cuneiform?"

"Maybe even proto-proto-proto." Betty handed another heavily marked photo to Julia. "What do you see here?"

"Looks ... pictographic?"

"Correct. Given this, we can assume some members of that early tribe took a detour and potentially wound up around what eventually became ancient Egypt. Some trekked through Eurasia—there are characters that resemble neolithic Chinese characters. I have another sample that looks astonishingly like ancient Norwegian runes. But when the Phoenicians came through and changed everything up, a lot of those early languages were impacted. Some died out."

"While the blast radius, for lack of a better term, to decipher cuneiform was largely limited to Persia and ancient Babylon ... "

Betty's smile was wide. "Exactly. The Quondan language has a much broader blast radius. Which is both bad and good. And it's where Francois has been helping us. You have to be careful, making side by side comparisons of languages. It can lead to a whole lot of bad assumptions. But he's been working with us to create a program that cross references the Quondan characters we have against several dictionaries worth of other ancient languages—cuneiform, obviously, but also Egyptian, Sumerian, Urartian, Assyrian, Minoan-Mycenean —you name it. As we get more samples, the translation program will become smarter."

Julia sat back in her chair and arched an eyebrow. "Lots to learn here."

“It’ll help you when you start working with Reg and Mari. Trust me.”

“That’s my next stop.”

Julia said her goodbyes and headed down the hall to the breakroom to meet the two people in charge of map making at the IFDC. She entered the room and cleared her throat. “Reginald Mountbatten, I presume?”

The resident map expert very nearly startled out of his skin and came perilously close to spilling the milk he was adding to his espresso.

“That’s me,” he said, straightening.

She smiled and extended her hand. “Julia Bassi.”

“A pleasure to finally make your acquaintance, Julia. Please, call me Reg.”

Reg was well over six feet, and his dark hair was arranged in thin, neat dreadlocks that fell to just past his shoulders. He wore a close-cut beard and tortoiseshell glasses.

“Harry asked me to make the rounds and meet everyone today. I can come back if the timing isn’t right.”

He took a sip from his mug and breathed a relieved sigh. “No, Dr. Bassi. Your timing is perfect.

Marisol pulled out a chair for Julia to sit in front of a screen Reginald was turning so they could all see it.

“It goes without saying,” Reginald explained, “that this is, has been, and will continue to be a ridiculously complicated undertaking.”

“That’s our Reg,” Marisol remarked dryly. “A master of understatement.”

The screen in front of them showed one of several photographs from inside the pyramid. The image quality was poor, to say the least. “Here’s where our work began.”

“What are we looking at?” Julia asked.

He shrugged his shoulder before answering. “Generally speaking, we believe this right here”—he tapped the screen to enlarge a corner of it—“is a map. Specifically, we are not yet sure what it is a map of. In fact, we have been asking ourselves that rather a lot lately." Reg shrugged. "It could be a map, some kind of mural, or an ancient recipe for Yorkshire pudding."

"Definitely not," Marisol said. "Too far from Yorkshire."

He sighed. "True. Not even accounting for continental drift would change that."

"He's only half-kidding," Marisol said. "Part of the problem with ancient cartography is the way things are presented; the maps are so old the landscape no longer resembles it anymore. Consequently, we have shapes in these maps that could indicate a body of water, but no way to tell if it's meant to be an ocean or an incredibly large lake. We've been working with Dr. Faulkner to craft a key for the image."

"Because you see," Reg added, pointing to the screen, "some of these little hatch marks could indicate a forest, or it could be a word. A warning. 'Beware: snakes.'"

"'Here be monsters,'" Marisol added. "All kidding aside, though, this is the process. We aren't even at step one. It's step zero."

"The first step, then, is to clean it up," Julia said.

"Which I'm thrilled to report my colleague began yesterday."

Marisol nodded and clicked a button to progress to the next image. "This is as far as I've gotten."

The graininess snapped into focus. Even some of the gloom of the cave had been brightened.

"That's amazing," Julia murmured.

"If only the process took a click or two on a keyboard," Reg murmured. "It takes time and impressively strong GPUs to pull this off. I'm going to assume you've yet to visit the servers."

"Correct," Julia said. "That's later."

"Give yourself plenty of time. There's a lot there. And Monsieur Severeux is enthusiastic about his work."

Marisol nodded avidly. "The processing power is off the charts—and between the machine learning, AI, and large language models, this place needs every ounce. I won't bore you with the ins and outs of how our program works, but Francois and his team have been instrumental in getting things just right."

Reginald pointed at the screen. "However, back to the process. You can see it looks a bit more map-like now. Could also still be a mural. Or Yorkshire pudding. Cartography is rather a dead art, these days. Nobody makes maps anymore, not really. Not like they used to."

"For most projects—this isn't our first—Reg and I work together; he's the expert on ancient maps, and I'm the expert on obtaining physical information from an environment through the use of photographic images."

"Okay ... " Julia looked between them. "I'm probably oversimplifying this but let me take a stab at it. You"—she looked at Reg—"understand the ancient maps; you know everything about maps, and you,"—she looked at Marisol—"understand how to convey that information using photos of a geological area."

"Yes," Reg said. "Maps as we know them are a representation of space. But over time, geography changes. Especially over hundreds of thousands of years. Mari and I are working together to create a modern representation of the map in question."

"I've been running simulations to determine how landmasses may have looked a hundred thousand years ago. With luck, our Eemians were sticklers for details."

"Meanwhile, I go back through the classics and the masters. Early maps made areas of importance appear larger than places that might have been physically larger. Have they done that here? No way to tell yet."

Julia nodded. "And you hope to meet in the middle?"

Reg gave her a blank look. "No. We've made a wager. The loser carries the winner's luggage at the next conference we attend."

20

The only thing worse than having no money, Magnus learned after too many expensive conversations with a lawyer who charged by the second, was having money that he couldn't touch.

Or, rather, money that would be parceled out slowly, over the span of months, years—not quickly enough to save him, to save Empire, to patch all the holes in the sinking ship. Money that depended on keeping his wayward son in check, sitting behind an Empire desk where he belonged.

Magnus glanced down at the locked drawer. He could practically feel the cold weight of metal against his hand, against the roof of his mouth. He clenched his jaw. *You're weak, boy. You've always been weak.*

Magnus wasn't even sure which path was the weak one anymore. He clenched his hand into a fist, steeling himself for what he needed to do.

And then, he reached for the phone.

"Well, well, well," said Tommy Jones on the other end of the line. "If it ain't Magnus Sawyer."

Magnus's spine stiffened and he tightened his grip on the phone to keep from hanging up like he wanted to. "Tommy," he said. "How've you been keeping?"

Tommy's laugh was as grating as ever. "I don't think so, Magnus. As I recall, the last time we spoke, you told me, and I quote, 'You're a bottom-feeding monster, Tommy, and if you ever so much as think about me again, I'll'—what was it? Have me fed to your dogs or buried in an oil well? Something melodramatic. Imagine my surprise when your number pops up just now."

Magnus adopted his most ingratiating, placating tone. "Now, Tommy, that's all in the past. I was havin' a real rough go of it, and I see now I took it all out on the wrong man."

"So, you're not knocking on my metaphorical door to ask me to, once more, pull your sorry ass out of the fire in which you've sat?"

"You've got me there, Tommy. You surely do. But the thing is—it's not so much pullin' me out of a fire as ... well, as it's me comin' to you with a real fine business opportunity."

Tommy's bark of laughter was so sharp and loud that Magnus had to pull the phone away from his ear. "That'd be a first."

Magnus's tongue stuck to the roof of his mouth. When he reached for words, they faded into dust before he could speak them.

"But," added Tommy, "even a stopped clock is right twice a day. Maybe I'll hear you out."

God Himself descending from the heavens couldn't have filled Magnus with more relief than these words Tommy delivered. The feeling of metal in his mouth disappeared, and he said, "I need to run an idea by you. It's big. Bigger 'n the both of us."

"Sounds like a conversation we should have over lunch," Tommy purred. "The club? I'm on the front nine."

Magnus had the presence of mind to wait a moment before agreeing; he didn't want to sound as desperate as he felt. When he hung up the phone, he placed his left hand atop his right to steady it. Confidence was critical. Tommy Jones might have his balls in a vise, but Magnus would be damned before he flinched. He swiveled his chair to face the window. Wavy lines of morning heat and humidity blurred the reddish-brown haze of pollution blanketing the Dallas skyline. It would be close to ninety degrees outside already, and it would feel hotter what with the humidity as the flooding from the devastating hurricane south of them slowly evaporated.

Magnus crossed his office to the wood-slatted closet door and stepped inside. Freshly pressed golf shirts in white, yellow, blue, and pink hung from a four-foot rod. He chose yellow. Positive. Optimistic. He looked at his watch. He'd have to hurry.

Magnus raced to the club, stole a parking spot from someone already waiting with their blinker flashing, and flung himself into a waiting golf cart.

"Mr. Jones and his party just teed off at the ninth hole," said a young caddy. "If you're ready, sir, I'll take you there now."

They bounced past dark green fairways pockmarked with white sand traps, stopping to wait whenever a golfer prepared to swing.

"That's them up ahead," said the caddy.

Magnus blinked in surprise when he realized Tommy wasn't golfing with one of his usual crowd of interchangeable hundred-dollar-haircut business-types. Today, his partner was a woman with legs a mile long and blonde hair in a jaunty ponytail. She also wore a yellow polo, but Magnus had to admit she filled hers out a hell of a lot more attractively than he did.

Magnus had composed himself by the time Tommy and the woman finished their putts on the ninth. By the time they reached their cart, Magnus was already standing there, hand extended.

Tommy's handshake was just a little too firm. Don't flinch. Magnus forced himself to smile. Tommy nodded as though Magnus had passed some kind of test. "I know you're not a golfing man, Magnus, so I won't ask you to join us for the back nine. How's about we break for lunch? I could go for a steak so blue it still moos when I cut into it."

The visual turned Magnus's stomach, but he laughed because he knew Tommy expected him to.

"Magnus, you ever met Jacqueline Henley?" Tommy asked, indicating his golf partner.

Magnus shook his head before offering his hand once again. The woman was even more of a stunner up close and personal. Though her skin was soft, her handshake was perfect—just the right amount of pressure, and not too long or too short.

"Jack," said Jacqueline Henley in a voice as rich and smooth as chocolate mousse. "Only my mama calls me Jacqueline—and that's when she's mad."

Magnus couldn't quite place her accent. *Rich,* he thought. *And used to getting whatever she wants.* Hell, he was half ready to give her the moon if she asked him for it.

"Jack's got some connections," Tommy said. He didn't bother hiding his smirk when he glanced between her and Magnus. Then he brushed his thumb across his fingertips in the universal gesture for cold hard cash. "When you called me up just now, we got to talkin'—and I think maybe you want her to sit in on our little lunch, too."

Jack settled her golf-gloved hand on Magnus's forearm and turned a thousand-watt smile his way. Magnus couldn't place her age—anywhere from thirty to fifty, and gorgeous no matter what.

Tommy said, "Takes a lot of grease to spin the wheels as need spinnin', these days. Not as easy as when your daddy ran Empire."

"Nothing is," Magnus said.

Jack laughed. "You can say that again. And twice on Sundays."

"Too early for a whiskey?" said Tommy with a wink.

"Hell," added Jack, "I'd say it's late enough for two."

They rode their carts to the club's restaurant and followed their hostess to a table near the south windows, overlooking the eighteenth hole. The wood-paneled walls and carved trim of the quiet dining room reminded Magnus of the many hours he'd spent in its warmth and comfort over the years. He was more at home here than in the big old house that had belonged to his daddy.

Over drinks and lunch, Magnus laid out Ethan Pickens's proposal. He slid the prepared brief across the table. In it, Pickens explained the Rulison Project and the expected gas yields. He'd also included topographical maps of the area, a budget, and a funding proposal.

Tommy rattled the ice cubes in his glass and knocked back the whiskey before setting it down on the table.

"This is the craziest-ass proposal I ever heard," he said as he tapped his finger on the papers. "But it might just be crazy enough to pique my interest."

Magnus sucked in a long inhale and tried his best not to smile.

"Let me run it by a few engineers I trust, and we'll talk again. Fair enough?"

Magnus nodded his head.

"Jack," said Jones, "weren't you saying you wanted a moment to freshen up?"

She'd said no such thing, but she smiled and rose from the table all the same.

As soon as Jack left, Tommy snapped his fingers. The young waitress scurried to the table.

"Two more of these, honey." He winked. "Best be tall and straight up. My friend here's thirsty." Tommy's eyes remained fixed on her ass as she headed back to the bar. Magnus cleared his throat.

"Magnus," Tommy continued, still watching the waitress. "You and I both know you wouldn't be here, talkin' to me, if things weren't real desperate for you."

The flare of hope punched through Magnus like a bullet. "It is, Tommy. There's nothing even close, why—"

Tommy put up his hand. "I don't need a sales pitch. That's Jack's department."

Stung by the dismissal, Magnus nodded.

"What I do need is loyalty. Trust. Am I making myself clear?"

Magnus nodded again.

"Just so there's no misunderstanding, old friend—if I do this, and by the looks of this proposal I am thinkin' real hard that might just happen—you're all in. Lock, stock, and barrel. Everything." Before Magnus could ask what 'everything' might entail, Tommy leaned forward, eyes narrowed. "I say jump, you ask how high. And when it comes to business, I want you seen and not heard. You got lots goin' for you, Magnus Sawyer, but a head for business just ain't one of them."

Magnus nodded, but Tommy raised expectant eyebrows.

After a dry swallow, Magnus said, “Anything you say, Tommy.”

Tommy smiled, slow as the Cheshire Cat and twice as ghastly. “And I don’t want to hear a single disparaging word about me, about my methods, about the way I’m gonna run things. And I am, Magnus. I am going to *run things.* If I so much as catch you frowning at me, the deal’s off. I pull the money and take every damn thing you own to offset the interest you’ll owe me.”

The chill that ran the length of Magnus’s spine had nothing at all to do with the blasting air conditioning. *You’re getting’ into bed with the devil, my boy.*

Magnus stuck out his hand before he could think twice. “Then we have a deal.”

The waitress returned with their drinks. She didn’t meet Tommy’s eyes, and she didn’t linger.

Tommy raised his glass and inhaled its scent. “I’d say say maybe. Maybe we have a deal. I still need to run it by my engineers. But, if we do this,” he said, pinning Magnus beneath a predator’s glare, “I want there to be no questions between us. You fuck with me, question me, or even *think* about taking me for a ride, old friend, and I’ll see you planted next to your daddy.”

Tommy held out his glass for Magnus to toast, and he smiled when Magnus’s tumbler tapped the side of his own.

21

IFDC Headquarters

Days turned into weeks. Julia met regularly with each team lead, but breakthroughs were a rare commodity.

She knew—as did everyone else in the IFDC—that research was very frequently a slog. Lightning-bolt moments were few and far between. Patience and perseverance had to be everyone's watchwords.

One benefit was that living in a dormitory environment brought them closer as a unit; they worked together; they ate meals together in the galley; they even enjoyed the occasional "movie night" and worked out in the facility's gym together. Reginald taught Sky tricks—apparently his family back in England bred dogs and he was grateful for the distraction.

Sky, in fact, integrated well. He had his favorites—Shannon was at the top of the list because she ran errands and usually came armed with dog treats, but Sky could often be found napping on one of the couches in the linguistic department. Whenever someone attempted to shoo him off the furniture, Dr. Faulkner said the same thing: "Sky lowers my stress level; remove him from the furniture only if you believe you can do the job half as well as he."

One evening, after a long run on the treadmill, Julia was on her way back to her dormitory, Sky on her heels, when her cell phone rang. It was Reginald.

She didn't even get the chance to say hello.

"I have searched every square inch of this labyrinth. Where in bloody blue blazes are you?"

She arched an eyebrow at his tone but didn't comment on it. "About to hit the showers, what's going on?"

"Don't bother with the shower. Marisol and I have something. Come now."

The IFDC conference room crackled with an energy that wasn't just from the humming servers lining the walls. Monitors and keyboards lay scattered like the relics of a digital Stonehenge across the imposing oak table, smothered in maps and dog-eared notebooks. Above them a pair of colossal video screens held a captive audience. Even Sky seemed to be staring at the map's image Reginald had posted.

"Now, what you have to remember about ancient maps," Reginald said, every word, every gesture buzzing with excitement, "is that they were seldom accurate. The more important a location was, the larger it appeared on a map, for example. Actual size had nothing to do with it, largely because at the time nobody knew how to calculate it."

"Right," Julia said, reaching down to pet Sky's head. "Early maps conveyed cultural information more than they gave an idea of land mass size."

"Until Ptolemy," Reginald said, holding up one finger.

"Ptolemy changed everything," Marisol said, nodding. "He was the first to successfully estimate land mass. No one else before then had the skill—or understanding."

"He was also the first to use lines of longitude and latitude," Reginald said, crossing the room to stand by a detailed replica of an ancient map on the wall—a reproduction of Ptolemy's *Geographia.*

"His precision was remarkable for the age. And withstood the test of time—it's not exact by our standards, but there are remarkably few errors. He laid the groundwork for cartography as we know it."

"Reg, now show Julia what we found," Marisol said. Reginald looked pained.

"What's wrong?" Julia asked.

"He's annoyed it took us this long to see it."

"It was staring us right in the bloody face the whole while," he grumbled, walking to his computer.

"What was?" Julia asked.

Reginald shook his head, addressing Marisol instead. "You show her what you found first."

With a sigh, Marisol brought her computer display to life, revealing what appeared to be a satellite image—islands, archipelagoes, and large swaths of land, cut here and there by rivers and mountain ranges. "This is what landmasses looked like a hundred thousand years ago."

Julia tilted her head, trying to see any resemblance to modern-day continents and countries, but could not.

Marisol read the confusion in Julia's face. "No, it really doesn't look like much of anything familiar. It's a little like Pangaea but not quite. But wait." She hit a sequence of keys on the keyboard. "And watch."

Julia watched as the unfamiliar landmass drifted apart, breaking into more familiar formations. A timeline ran across the bottom of the screen. Marisol stopped the simulation again and Julia's eyes went to the bottom of the screen. Even Sky sat up and took notice.

"Twelve thousand years ago," Julia said quietly.

"Bingo," Marisol replied. "Probably about when our Antarctic friends first started poking their heads above ground."

"Remember what that looks like," Reginald said, taking a seat at his workstation, Sky following him, curiously. He pulled up an image of the Eemian cave wall—the refinement process had progressed leaps and bounds since the first time Julia looked at it. The cave wall very clearly depicted a map now.

"Definitely not Yorkshire pudding," Julia murmured as Sky started wagging his tail. The dog pranced over to Julia, shoving his head under her hands. She scratched his ears but did not pull her attention away from the cave wall image. Sky wiggled more insistently against her, and she looked down. His mouth was open in a canine grin, and she smiled in return. "Yes, it's good news, isn't it?"

Reginald chuckled. "That it's not Yorkshire pudding is the one thing we're certain of. Now, what do you see?"

Julia looked back and forth between Marisol's simulation and the cave wall.

"I see no similarity at all. Should I?"

"No," he replied, flatly.

Julia blinked. "Wait, what?"

Reginald pushed away from his computer and walked back to the framed replica of Ptolemy's map. "Look here. What do you see here?"

Julia got up and walked closer, eyes narrowing. She looked over at the cave map and back again. "Can anyone tell me why the cave wall that predates Ptolemy bears such a striking resemblance to Ptolemy's map?"

"No," Marisol said. "More to the point, it shouldn't. At no point during the time the Eemians existed did land masses look anything like that," she said, nodding at the map on the wall.

"Now, if you look closely, the Eemian map is ... a little more loosely presented," Reginald said. "A bit more abstract." He walked back to his computer, gesturing at the screen. "Almost like an early iteration. A beta version, if you will."

Marisol joined him. "It's as if Ptolemy improved upon the ... the wildness of the original, crafting something more precise."

Reginald traced the signs with a fingertip. "The shapes on this earlier representation—these circles, triangles, and curves, all interconnect in a way that, if nothing else, hints at an underlying logic. As I've mentioned, the landmasses here are markedly more abstract rather than realistic. However, their placement and proportion suggest a surprising—for the time—understanding of spatial relationships." He pointed to a series of concentric circles dominating a segment of the cave wall map. "And here—these markings appear to pre-date Greek cartography by a significant margin."

"And these lines look as if they might correlate with specific positions," Marisol said. "Possibly locations."

As Julia looked closer at the cave wall image, Sky pressed to her side. Could he sense her own rising excitement? "Are you telling me you think the Eemians had their own way of mapping the world?" she asked. "A way that ... Ptolemy somehow figured out?"

"That does seem to be the size of it," Reginald said.

Marisol shook her head, looking back at her simulation. "What I don't understand is how the Eemians knew what the landscape would look like before it ever looked that way. We were looking too far back, never figuring the Eemians had the technology to look forward."

"At any rate, what we did next was overlay the Eemian map with Mari's simulations. We both saw there was a pattern, an order to the chaos."

Marisol ran another simulation, a partially transparent overlay of the Eemiam map on top of the shifting landmasses. "Francois wrote a program that identified shapes on the Eemian map, correlating to the shapes that come up in the simulation."

"Painfully long story made bearably short," Reginald said, "it's Norway."

"Norway," Julia echoed. Adrenaline buzzed in her veins. "It's Norway? Really?" She swallowed hard. *Get a grip, Bassi.* "Okay. There's still a lot of country to narrow down, though. Right?"

Reginald and Marisol exchanged a look. "Do you want to tell her," Mari said, "or shall I?"

"Oh, let me," Reg replied, looking like the cat that ate the canary. "Stars."

"Beg pardon?" Julia blurted.

"How the sailors of old found their way across the seas," he said, growing more excited. Sky pranced to his side, his body moving from side to side with the force of his tail-wags. "These lines connect stars."

"You're telling me these points and lines on the cave wall image represent the exact position of the stars from where the Eemians hid their sanctuaries?" Julia stopped suddenly and shook her head. "But the skies—stars and constellations change over time. How do we—"

This time Marisol grinned. "It so happens that Francois wrote us a program for *that,* too. I'm still running the simulations." She paused. "But for the first time in a while, I'm optimistic."

22

Word spread quickly through the IFDC, and within two or three hours, the conference room was abuzz. Team leads and their assistants filled seats—everyone had been pulled from various tasks, from workout sessions, like Julia, to mealtimes. Dr. Faulkner sat at her table with a grilled cheese sandwich and cup of tomato soup. Harry sat next to her with a cup of coffee, nibbling on a chocolate bar.

It had taken some convincing to get Reginald to accept taking center stage to explain this particular revelation. Julia couldn't understand why—he seemed to be a natural in front of the group.

"If you will, Dr. Gutierrez?" he asked.

Mari nodded and tapped a series of keys on her laptop. The screens ringing the room came to life. The first image on the screen was the high-resolution image that had started out as the blurry background in a poorly lit smartphone photo.

"I'm sure by now we're all familiar with some iteration of this image. And," he said, nodding to Mari, "there is a chance some of you might also be familiar with this one."

Mari hit another sequence of keys, and the image of the Ptolemy map replaced that of the cave wall. A murmur rippled through the room, and Julia looked over at Harry to catch her reaction.

Harry smiled.

The next image displayed on the screen was a semi-transparent Eemian map superimposed over the Ptolemy.

"Well, I will be damned," Harry said quietly. "It's—that's *Norway.*"

Nodding, Julia said, "Of the two sanctuaries we've already unearthed, one is in Greenland and the other in Antarctica—poles apart but similar in their remoteness from what we know must have been the equatorial furnace of a hundred thousand years ago. Land-based, isolated, and inhospitable to most but perhaps a sanctuary to some. Norway makes sense if we assume that these sanctuaries would be as far away from the equator as possible and located on land masses."

"Dr. Bassi is correct," Reg said. "However, there was a portion of the Eemian map we still couldn't decode." The next image showed a section of the cave wall, enlarged even more. "Putting aside the fact that cave-dwellers produced a map of Ptolemy's level of accuracy, this"—Reginald gestured to the screen—"confounded us until very recently."

Mari advanced the slide again. Another image filled the monitors: dots of varying sizes and colors appeared on a dark grid; lines connected them into different shapes, forming geometric figures in three-dimensional space.

"Say hello to an Eemian sky, after a fashion," Reginald announced. Another murmur, this time louder, moved through the room like a wave. He waited for the noise to die down before adding, "The key to this map isn't terrestrial. It's celestial. They knew thousands of years ago what explorers didn't figure out until thousands of years later: Navigation via the stars."

The image advanced yet again, showing a series of Eemian language characters. "Thanks to Dr. Faulkner, we have a rough translation of this portion of the map."

"A rough, *incomplete* translation," Dr. Faulkner corrected them.

Harry waved a hand. "It's more than we had a month ago. So, what's the basic gist?"

Betty put down her sandwich. "The most important words in that bit of text are 'light,' something that is either 'hide' or 'hidden,' and something that suggests either ... payment, or sacrifice, or some kind of offering. I don't have enough information to build context for that last one. I don't know if we're supposed to make an offering or if the thing that they're calling light is meant to be an offering to us. It could be either at this point. I also need more context clues to determine whether this use of 'light' indicates the Power of the Light."

The room went eerily quiet.

Harry's voice cut through the silence. "Reg, Mari, have you identified those star patterns and verified they are indeed what you suggest?"

Marisol stood. "Yes. I've run most of the simulations. We have a match. It's important to bear in mind that stars and constellations change over time. Even the Earth's poles aren't fixed—those shift as well. In the same way that continents drift, volcanoes erupt, archipelagoes form, and islands are swallowed up with water, so too do stars form and die out, and a hundred other factors. A star's light that hadn't yet reached the Eemians may well have just reached our sight today. As such, we had to work backward until we reached a point in time that matched these constellations." She tapped a few keys and brought up the star map again. We've found the Eemian map's version of the sky, so to speak."

"And?" Harry prompted.

"We have a map, we have stars, and we have a grid. Effectively, we have a celestial longitude and latitude." He smiled. "With those we can find anything."

"Even hidden sanctuaries?" Harry prompted.

"Even those," Reg replied.

Lily Harrington pushed her thick-rimmed glasses up the bridge of her nose and stood.

"Maybe I can help. You see, I ... I don't think this is just a map."

"Lily," Harry said, "what do you mean by 'not just a map'?"

"Given Dr. Faulkner's preliminary translation, it would not surprise me if there's a ... a catch, so to speak. The use of the word hidden suggests that we have to find the hidden thing. It does depend on whether the actual context for the final word is offering or sacrifice, however. If it is in fact sacrifice, things could potentially get complicated." She paused. "Er. More complicated."

"Thank you, Lily. That's something to keep in mind," said Harry, turning her gaze toward Julia, Al, and Mari. "So, what's next?"

Dr. Faulkner stood. "Reg, Mari, could you please pull up the image with the ... let's call it a riddle for now."

In just a few seconds the screens glowed with Eemian characters. Betty folded her arms and frowned up at the screen. "The next step," she said, "is to decipher this. If we can get the translation down to beyond a shadow of a doubt, even better. Supposing Lily's right and it's a riddle—and it certainly could be, given what little we do know, then this section here needs to be coherent."

Julia nodded. "We're narrowing down the details of our destination. The next step is to figure out what to do once we get there."

Harry stood, her chair scraping the floor. "Lily, I want you to keep in contact with Betty's linguistics team. Stay in the loop, in the event we are looking at some kind of riddle or code."

"Got it," Lily said, smiling at Betty.

"James, see what you and your team have—or can find—on ancient Norwegian settlements, early villages, that sort of thing. There may be local legends or lore we can make practical use of."

James gave a brief salute and closed his laptop.

"Mari, you and Reg keep hammering away at that map. Once that simulation's done, let us know and we'll move forward. In the meantime, I'm going to touch base with some of my contacts in that part of the world and see if I can learn anything useful."

There was a flurry of activity as everyone began gathering up their belongings, but Harry's voice cut through the din.

"One last thing, everyone. I've been part of projects before that seemed godsent, only to see the fruits of our labor weaponized, privatized, or simply buried to protect existing power structures. No matter how we proceed, we will need to be careful."

Julia thought suddenly of Uzziel and barely suppressed her shudder.

23

Houston, Texas, Twenty Years Earlier

Magnus Sawyer checked again to make sure the hotel's bathroom door was locked before pulling from his briefcase a bottle of *No Gray Quick Fix* hair dye. With a few careful caresses, the spindly mascara-like brush teased out a hint of gray just above his ears. He moved to within inches of the mirror so he could see only his face, then lifted his upper lip's left corner to expose the slight color differences between his canine and two new premolars. Unacceptable. He'd have to make an appointment to fix that. He let his lip go and patted his hair in place. Satisfied, he unlocked the door and entered the dark, wood-paneled hall where his wife Susan was anxiously waiting.

"Everything okay?" she asked.

Magnus again lightly patted his hair and smiled yes.

The phone in his suit's breast pocket vibrated. He didn't bother to pull it out. No doubt another reminder from Mrs. Langham that his guests were waiting.

"Is Sam here?" he asked.

She pointed down the hall at a skinny sixteen-year-old standing next to the hors d'oeuvres table in the main room.

Magnus grabbed Susan's hand and together they stepped into the cavernous meeting room of the Intercontinental Hotel.

A tall well-dressed man moved out of the crowd and swaggered toward them. "Magnus, you old son of a bitch."

Susan squeezed his hand and whispered "He's all yours" before heading alone to the cocktail bar.

"Dan!" Magnus grinned. "I swear you can strut sittin' down. Look at you, sir!"

Dan's long, stoic face suddenly broke into a smile that left his cheeks rose-colored. Or maybe that was the open bar. Either way.

"Thanks for coming, Dan. Did you bring the boys?"

"Hell, Magnus, not only did I bring the boys, I managed to get Tommy Jones himself to join us."

"Jones?" asked Magnus.

"Yup. Tommy "President of the Texas Mid-Continent Oil and Gas Association" Jones, in the flesh. He should be here any time."

The ninth-floor meeting room was filling up quickly. Magnus and Dan both ordered double Wild Turkeys, neat. The two made their way toward a group of three men in dark suits and polished cowboy boots standing next to the room's lavishly curtained floor-to-ceiling windows. After the requisite hand-shaking and back-slapping of old friends, Magnus's attention drifted to the view outside those windows.

"It never ceases to amaze me," muttered Magnus as he gazed at the massive Texas Medical Center's campus.

The four turned toward the window.

"See that parking structure just to the north of that big building?" asked Magnus. "That used to be the old Shamrock Hotel. Biggest in the world. Now, it's just a damned parking lot."

"Fitting for Houston," snarked the man closest to him.

"That hotel was magnificent," said Magnus. "Had the world's

biggest swimming pool. Big enough they had a motorboat pulling water skiers doing laps behind it."

One of the four whistled.

"Greatest man that ever lived owned that hotel," continued Magnus. "Glen McCarthy. A bigger-than-life Texan—and ain't that saying something. An oil driller like us. The kind they don't make anymore."

"Did you ever meet him?" asked John.

Magnus smiled and shook his head. "My daddy and Glen were friends. 'Bout ten years before they tore down that hotel, the three of us had lunch together there. I was just a kid and never said a word."

Dan nodded.

"That man, Glen?" added Magnus as he stared off into the distance. "At one time, he was the richest man in the world. He and Howard Hughes were pals. Hell, Hughes gave Glen a million-dollar airplane just for being his buddy."

"Whatever happened to McCarthy?" asked one of the three.

Magnus clenched tight his jaw and shook his head. "Same thing that could happen to any of us, Mike. Got his finances twisted around, couldn't get enough capital to keep drilling the wells growing our country. Banks screwed him out of everything. He lost it all."

Dan nodded. "Bastards."

Magnus's breast pocket phone vibrated for the second time in less than a minute. He searched the room until his eyes locked on to Mrs. Langham's short frame standing near the entrance to the meeting room. She was pointing at her watch and then with a wave of her hand, urged him to approach the small podium at the far wall.

"Thank you all for being here," Magnus spoke into the microphone. "First, I want to welcome all my friends and colleagues—" He paused, then turned his attention to the room's back corner, where Susan and Sam were standing. "But before I get in trouble, I better include in that welcome my lovely new bride, Susan, and the future CEO of Empire Oil, my son, Sam."

There was a small round of polite applause.

"What a treat to be hosting this important fundraiser for my alma mater, Rice University. We are honored by our guests today." Magnus looked toward a group of men standing next to the bar. "A special welcome to Congressmen Adams, Hindley, and Robbins."

The room broke out in a loud round of applause.

"Now you boys take care around that open bar," he chuckled. "Wouldn't want to get you all liquored up before heading back to Austin—unless, of course, you're willing to see things the way we oilmen do."

Magnus clapped as the crowd laughed.

"And a special welcome to my good friends from the Texas Mid-Continent Oil and Gas Association. Now, I expect you boys to open your wallets wide for this noble cause."

There was a round of applause and the four moved away from the windows and closer to the podium.

"Now, before I introduce our guest of honor, Dr. Robert Esposito, President of Rice University, I want to share a story with you all."

There were groans and laughter from the crowd.

"Now, now." Magnus chuckled and patted the air in front of him for quiet. "I'll keep her short."

Hoots and howls erupted in the room.

Undaunted, Magnus continued. "I was just telling the boys that not too long ago, my father, Henry and I were having lunch with one of the wealthiest men in the world. Glen McCarthy, an oil man like many of us in this room."

"Glen and my father were men's men. Salt-of-the-Earth, red-blooded Americans who felt the only work worth doing was done with their own hands. They built this great nation of ours, a country that is today, I am sorry to say, is in a serious heap of trouble."

There were nods and grunts of acceptance from the audience.

"Seems everybody today's got somethin' to say whether any good or not comes from them sayin' it. Here in Texas, we're not about to give way to all this liberal horseshit some folks want spread around."

Magnus beamed his approval as the crowd broke into laughter.

"We gotta saying here in Texas, be thankful we're not getting all the government we're paying for."

The three congressmen looked directly at Magnus.

"Present company excepted," he added.

Behind the crowd the clink of plates and glasses peppered the air as the wait staff prepped the rows of small round white tables for dinner.

"When my lovely new bride, Susan, started workin' on me to gather our industry friends and colleagues to help raise enough money for a new science wing at Rice, I shook my head no. No. Enough of all this new-fangled oil-drilling equipment the science boys keep cookin' up. Help me out here. What do they call this new sideways drilling?"

"Fracking!" one of the three lobbyists blurted out.

Magnus nodded. "Yup, that's what they call it alright. But bless her heart, Susan stayed on me until I remembered something my daddy, Henry used to say. He said, 'Magnus, my boy, there's two theories about how to argue with a woman and win. Neither one works.'"

Now the crowd applauded and laughed.

"Seriously, we are here today to open our wallets to help our friends at Rice University.

"What I have come to learn is that science is inevitable. Men like my father and Glen McCarthy dug Texas gold out of the earth with their bare hands. But if today's oilmen are gonna have any chance of competing with the likes of those folks at OPEC killing our economy, we gotta outsmart them. Outthink them. And to do that, we need to support science and trust in these youngsters coming up through the ranks."

Magnus reached under the podium's top, pulled out his glass of Wild Turkey, and held it high.

"I am asking each and every one of you for two favors. First, open your wallets and give as generously as you are able. Susan and I have kicked off this fundraiser by promising a very generous gift to our friends at Rice."

Magnus looked right at President Esposito, smiled, and winked. Esposito tipped his glass in a salute.

"Second, let's all drink to America. No matter what troubles her, she's still the greatest country in the world!"

24

Dallas, Texas

Magnus handed his rain-drenched overcoat to the woman at the coat check, pocketed the green plastic claim chip she gave him, and then followed the maître d' past candlelit tables. Rain hammered the roof of the Dallas Country Club with all the force of stampeding cattle.

Though Magnus had timed things so he would arrive early, Tommy had anticipated him. Seemed like Tommy was always anticipating him, these days. Hell, even though Tommy was just a loan shark, Magnus often felt that the greasy little man had gone and usurped his role as CEO of Empire without so much as a tip of the hat.

But he'd come through with the cash.

Work was already underway in Colorado, just as damn fast as money could pay for.

Jones sat alone at a small round table near the back of the club's dining area, an empty rocks glass in front of him.

"Ain't seen rain like this for some time," said Tommy.

Magnus removed his suit jacket and hung it over the back of the red velvet chair, refusing the maître d's offer of help. He waved a hand toward the exterior windows. "Suppose it's a good thing our Lord swore never to drown the world again, or I'd be worried."

The skies lit up, followed almost instantly by a roll of thunder loud enough to rattle the glasses on the tables around them. A woman seated nearby dropped her silverware. Tommy adjusted his napkin and smiled, his lean face and swept-back black hair lit by the yellow glow of the candle on the table.

"Thank you for joining me for dinner," said Tommy. "I know it was short notice."

Jump, you said, thought Magnus. *This is me asking "How high?"*

The waiter poured glasses of water and stood at attention.

"What'cha havin'?" asked Tommy. "Your favorite?"

Magnus smiled.

"Two glasses of your best Kentucky bourbon," Tommy ordered. "Each with two cubes."

"Certainly, Mr. Jones."

The waiter delivered the drinks and both men downed them before he left. Lifting two fingers, Tommy signaled for another round.

Magnus ignored the burn in his belly and kept his gaze fixed on Tommy.

"Your man, Ethan Pickens," Tommy began. "He's the real deal. Things are comin' together out there, Magnus. They're comin' together real fast." Tommy smacked his lips in a gross parody of satisfaction. "Using explosives to make our own little atomic bomb to frack gas out of the Green River Formation. It's genius."

Magnus realized he wasn't breathing and forced himself to exhale. The waiter set two more glasses of whiskey in front of them. Tommy slowly ran his index finger around the crystal rim of the glass, staring into the dark liquid.

"Crazy as it sounds," he continued, "we're gonna shoot that first shot in a couple-a months, tops."

Magnus gripped the small glass in his right hand and sucked a quiet breath into his lungs, not wanting to interrupt the wave of good fortune washing over him. They downed their drinks. The waiter hurried over, but Tommy's two fingers were quicker; the waiter did an about-face and scurried to the bar.

"You hungry?" asked Tommy.

He wasn't. He still had the wherewithal to know Tommy's question was rhetorical. Magnus and Tommy reached for their menus at the same moment. The lights in the restaurant flickered and the drone of pounding rain filled the silence between them.

"I don't know why I even bother lookin'," said Tommy, putting the leather booklet back on the table. "Been ordering the same thing for twenty years, and I ain't changing it tonight. Dry-aged T-bone seasoned with salt, pepper, and butter. Crunchy on top, bloody in the middle. Add one of them fresh rolls, lots of butter, and maybe a green bean or two, and I swear to God it's Heaven on Earth. You in?"

Magnus preferred his steak medium rare with the peppercorn sauce the kitchen here did so well, but he said nothing. *How high?*

They went through at least one more whiskey before the food arrived. When the waitstaff set white dinner plates heaped with food in front of them, Magnus had never been happier to see bread. He needed something to soak up the booze. Especially since Tommy showed no signs of slowing down. The sommelier poured a splash of red wine into Tommy's glass for his approval. The maître d' stood a few feet back from the table, the wait staff behind him, as Tommy pierced the steak with his fork, then slowly cut a slice with his knife. A pool of red dribbled onto the white plate, mingling with the green beans and yellow butter. He watched as Magnus did the same, and the two toasted each other.

The staff scattered. Magnus wished he could join them.

"Jack Henley, you remember her?"

Magnus thought a man would have to be blind to forget someone like Jack Henley, but he merely inclined his head.

"Jack's going to join us for a couple of drinks. You okay with that?"

How high? "Sure thing, Tommy."

"You're a good Christian—a God-fearing man. Am I right?"

"My faith's unshakable, Tommy."

"I know, old friend. What I don't know is your politics. You still a stand-up American? I seem to remember back twenty years or so when you gave a pretty good speech supporting our country. You still waving the flag?"

The rain intensified until it sounded less like a stampede and more like a whole damn army marching to war. Tommy poured the last of the red wine into Magnus's glass. Another clap of thunder, distant now, punctuated the moment.

"Wavin' it high and proud of it," said Magnus.

Tommy smiled, nodded, then turned his attention toward the restaurant's front entrance. "That's just what we wanted to hear," he said. He lifted a hand in greeting. "You make sure you spell that out for Jack, old friend. It's real important."

"Important?"

The room was spinning, and Magnus didn't think it only had to do with the amount of alcohol he'd drunk.

"Well, sure," said Tommy as Jack sauntered toward them. "She needs to know she can count on you."

Jacqueline Henley moved toward the table like she owned the place, and if Magnus had thought she looked good in her golfing get-up, it didn't hold a candle to her now. Her blonde hair fell in glossy waves around a face that belonged in magazines or on movie posters. Magnus and Tommy rose to greet her. Tall already, her jeweled stilettos gave her the advantage of height even over Magnus; Tommy had to tip his head back to meet her gaze. Not that he seemed to mind—at his height, he had a prime view of the assets revealed by a dress too perfectly tailored to be anything but stunning.

"Mr. Sawyer, Mr. Jones," said Jack. To Magnus, her voice sounded like sex and whiskey and the finest Cuban smoke. "I hope someone's already ordered a glass of whatever you've been enjoying for me. This weather's something else. There's talk that another hurricane's coming our way." She sat without even checking to make sure someone was holding her seat out for her.

Then again, a woman like her wouldn't spend a moment of her life doubting the effect she had on the men around her. The maître d' slid Jack's chair closer to the table and offered a menu that she waved away with a manicured hand. "No need, Charles," she said, offering him a smile. "The usual."

The maître d'—*Charles*—backed away from the table, half-bowing.

Jesus Christ, thought Magnus. *How long have I been coming here without once bothering to learn the man's name?*

Tommy's wry smile seemed to indicate that he was used to the ripple Jack left in her wake. "Sure hope we're not in for another drenching," Tommy said, returning to his seat. "That last one came through like a cattle stampede."

The waiter brought three fresh glasses and poured a bottle of newly decanted wine into them. They raised their glasses to toast. The first sip hit Magnus like a truck. The wine was rich, heady with age, and it probably cost more than all the rest of their evening's drinks put together.

Magnus hoped to the high heavens that he didn't get stuck with the bill. He wasn't sure he had a credit card with enough room on it.

Tommy leaned back in his chair like a presiding judge. Or maybe a monarch. "Jack, why don't you take it from here?"

Jack set down her glass and dabbed her red lips with a white linen napkin that came away snowy and unstained.

"There's more oil and gas in the Green River Formation than anywhere else in the world—enough to supply the entire planet for the next century." She tilted her head, casting half her face in shadows but letting the candlelight illuminate the golden waves of her hair. "But of course, you know that. With all this talk of climate change and global warming, who wouldn't jump at the chance to move this country away from oil and over to natural gas?"

"Exactly," said Tommy, picking up the patter like it was a bit he and Jack had polished before stepping out on stage. "Natural gas produces half as much CO_2 as coal or oil. A nation running entirely on natural gas would have half the emissions we're at now, slowing down this global warming business everyone's so agitated about." He winked at Magnus and Jack. "And if it makes the folks who pull it out of the ground a shitload of money in the process, well, who am I to complain?"

A sudden flash flooded the candlelit dining room with white light. A deep rumble followed a few seconds later.

"We can put Empire atop the heap by quietly gobbling up the available land leases in the Green River Formation before the rest of the industry gets wind of what we're up to," said Tommy. "Catch 'em off guard. If we follow the plan your boy Pickens has set out, Empire could be one of our country's top natural gas producers in five years' time. But we'll be makin' money in three."

Tommy again waved off the waiter and refilled the wine glasses himself.

"We've got the chance to put this country on track to becoming the leader in both energy and reducing emissions. We'd be setting an example for the rest of the planet." Tommy leaned forward. "There's only a few hitches in the git along. And that's where our Ms. Henley comes in."

Magnus raised his eyebrows. His head swam with liquor and the scent of Jack's perfume. "And if we're not *supplying* the energy, we're bending over for whoever is, and taking it up—" Magnus flushed. "Sorry about that, ma'am. Little rough with a lady present."

Jack's laugh was even better than her smile. "Nothing I haven't heard before, Mr. Sawyer. Hell, it's nothing I haven't said before, if I'm honest. The truth is, energy producers don't make the public's popularity list these days. Between the old BP spill in the Gulf, the massive flooding in downtown Miami, the recent hurricane that ripped through our state, and all this talk about the climate, fracking with explosives in our country's national parks and recreational areas is going to be a hard sell."

Magnus's stomach knotted so abruptly he had to swallow hard to keep all the booze he'd drunk where it belonged.

"Frankly, Magnus," Tommy said, "the company hasn't prospered since you took it over from your daddy. You let your boy and your crew walk all over you. Empire's financials are in the shitter. Worse than I thought, even."

Magnus bit the inside of lip and tried his best to swallow the rush of hot bile gathering in his throat. The tops of his cheeks were burning, and his vision blurred. Come hell or high water, he wasn't going to let the pair across the table see Magnus Sawyer cry. What would his daddy say now? He'd been through hard times before; this was yet another test of his strength.

Tommy had him in a vise and he could feel its jaws squeezing shut.

Magnus lifted his eyes from the tabletop to meet Tommy's, but Tommy looked down at Magnus's empty water glass. "I see you switched to water."

The rain outside lessened to a light sprinkle as the storm moved on. Magnus guessed it was close to midnight, but he didn't dare look at his watch for fear of displaying weakness.

"Magnus," said Tommy, "you understand the danger our country is in. The national debt is tremendous and growing faster than Texas turfgrass. We're at the mercy of China for that debt and the Middle East for our energy prices. The environmentalists and liberals want to turn off the oil spigot and return us to the Stone Age. We have never been as vulnerable as we are today. What we need is a champion to bring our country back to its roots, to its independent beginnings, to the glory days when the world looked up to America."

The three of them were all that remained of the club's evening dinner guests. The bartender was wiping down his area while the bussers cleared the tables of their dinner settings and prepped for breakfast. The lone remaining waiter brought a bottle of bourbon and three glasses to the table, which he filled.

Tommy emptied his glass and loudly set it down atop the table, then looked straight at Magnus. He lifted his glass to his lips with trembling hands and forced the burning amber liquid down.

Jack cleared her throat. She hadn't touched her glass of whiskey, but Tommy didn't seem to care. "Mr. Sawyer, if we're going to bring this country back to energy independence and stop falling behind on the world stage, to become the world's largest producer of clean natural gas, we need a leader. A front man who's going to make the world a better place and do it with a smile." She paused for what seemed like a millennium. "Mr. Sawyer, we believe you are that man."

Magnus froze.

Tommy refilled his glass and Magnus's and set the bottle down. "All you need do is what you're best at."

"And that is?"

"Glad-handin'," said Tommy. "No one's better than you at throwing a party, slapping people on the back, and making 'em feel good. Look, most of what we got to do is get people on our side. We need a friendly face to pitch the idea of doing what it takes to slow the pace of global warming with a new and energy efficient solution: natural gas. And if Empire just happens to be at the forefront of this solution, well, you're a family man, aren't you? A man of God. A true American."

"Bingo!" said Jack. The way her eyes lit up made Magnus want to do anything it took to keep her smiling. "That's what makes this work. Mr. Jones and I can handle the back end of this project. We can get the wells installed and start the gas flowing. Money can buy just about anything, and we need it to buy the goodwill of the people."

With embarrassment, he said, "Ma'am, you know damn well I haven't got two pennies to rub together until the well starts producing."

"We can fix that, Mr. Sawyer. Magnus. May I call you Magnus?" Her voice sounded positively sinful as it rolled through his name. He nodded dumbly, and he earned another of her smiles. "Because I have access to *plenty* of it. And my contacts have deep pockets and an interest in seeing Empire succeed."

Magnus's head spun in a way that had nothing to do with alcohol.

"I know this is a lot to take in, Magnus," said Jack, patting the back of his head. "Let me see if I can help you understand. Most people don't want change. Not really. They're looking for someone to wave a magic wand that makes this whole global warming business go away without having to change a single thing about their lifestyle." She smiled. "Americans love their cars. They love warm houses in winter and cool ones in the summer. They love all the conveniences that come with easy, cheap access to energy. They love these things so much that they don't want to think about the consequences of having them."

Jack sat back in her seat. Magnus immediately missed the warmth of her hand on his.

"You're not telling me anything I don't already know," he said. "Empire's built on it."

Jack nodded. "And don't we know it. See, here's where the problem starts. The environmentalists are pushing for change. Big change, like giving up our cars and our way of life. Monumental change. Truth be told, people just don't want to hear about it. They sure as hell don't want to feel bad about their choices. No one likes feeling guilty just for liking the things they like. They want the problem fixed with the least amount of effort on their part. And that's where you come in."

Magnus raised his eyebrows.

"You're a smiling Texas oil man offering his country an easy solution. One that won't require everyone changing their whole damn life. A few thousand camping nuts losing a place to park their tents is a hell of a lot easier for most Americans to swallow than windmills and solar panels in their backyard."

When she put it like that, Magnus could see it all so clearly.

"We all want clean energy," said Tommy, "but our world runs on fossil fuels. We can't just go cold turkey like those bleeding-heart idiots want us to. That's just plum nuts. And it asks too much of hard-working Americans. If these science dreamers ever figure out how to make cheap clean energy we can painlessly switch to, I'll be the first to support it, but until that happens, let's dig it out of the ground here and not be forced to import it from the Middle East or Canada.

Meanwhile, we're helping to save the planet by shifting away from the hard stuff."

"By switching to natural gas, we can cut this country's carbon load in half," Jack said in the easy, practiced voice of a professional spin doctor. Magnus had to hand it to her—she was damned good. She could probably sell air conditioning to an Eskimo. "That's nothing to sneeze at. You'd be a hero. Our country's hero."

A surge of confidence and energy welled up in Magnus. Now that he'd had a minute to let the proposal sink in, he could see the sense in it. He liked where it was going. Hell, he'd always been the first to admit that his daddy's way of doing things never sat right with him. He wasn't an oil man—he was a *people* man. A man of the people. A rush of adrenaline cut through the haze of alcohol. He searched their eyes for signs they were toying with him, but they seemed certain. Like they believed in what they were proposing.

"You gotta trust us," said Tommy. "It'll be a walk in the park for a guy like you. All you gotta do is smile. You're a God-loving Texas businessman hellbent on fixing climate problems while preserving the American way of life, helping America regain its world dominance as the energy leader, and raising the standard of living for every man and woman in our great country. Who can stand in your way?" With a white cloth napkin, Tommy wiped the spittle collecting around his mouth. "You just get out there and tell them the story they need to hear." Tommy poured what was left of the bourbon into their three glasses. "You in?"

Magnus picked up his glass.

"Trust me, Magnus, and I'll make you a rich man."

"More than that," Jack added. "We'll make you powerful."

They clinked their glasses together and knocked back the last of the bourbon.

25

Harry really had thought of everything. Even the basic human need for sunshine and fresh air.

Adjacent to the dormitories was a solarium/greenhouse that functioned as fully sustainable traditional and hydroponic vegetable gardens as well as an aesthetically pleasing flower garden. Julia didn't know the details about how the greenhouse stayed hidden from view, especially from aircraft or drones, but she was thankful for it.

She was especially thankful for it this evening as she and Sky walked along the winding stone path that twisted around plumeria trees and climbing night-blooming jasmine. The auto-waterers had gone off not long before and the garden air was damp and thick with the scent of tropical flowers. The perfect place to decompress. Sky's nose was glued to the ground, sniffing out every shred of cedar mulch, every hydrangea bloom, every leaf, and every new bud.

Julia remembered reading somewhere that dogs sniffed as a means to relieve stress; was that what Sky was doing now? *If that's the case, I can't blame you.*

They were so close. With every completed simulation, with every new round of translations, they were slowly zeroing in on where exactly they needed to go. Harry had already begun planning the expedition, which also took time, Julia knew. Things were moving quickly, compared to life in academia, but things weren't moving quickly *enough.*

Julia breathed in deeply and exhaled in a long sigh. Deep in the flower garden now, she folded her arms and turned in a slow circle. Cedar mulch twined with jasmine and frangipani. Breathing deeper, notes of basil and mint from the herb garden slipped in, adding a new dimension to the heady florals around her.

Nearly hidden beside a climbing honeysuckle was a wrought iron bench; honeysuckle and jasmine had started invading the bench's curlicues. Doubtless it would be cut back eventually but Julia couldn't help but admire the vine's natural instinct to stretch out and grow upon whatever surface presented itself.

Just then Julia's phone vibrated in her pocket. She pulled it out to see an unexpected but familiar name. She answered.

"You might be the last person I expected to hear from tonight, Grimes," she said.

"I do aspire to be a surprise whenever possible," he drawled. "How goes?"

"That's a hard one to answer. There's progress, just ... slow progress." She wrinkled her nose. "And that's not even accurate. Compared to how academic research goes, we're moving at practically MACH ten."

"But still not as fast as you'd like?" he asked.

"Right." Julia blew out a frustrated breath. "And what about you? Last I heard, you were ... " she trailed off, not sure how much to say.

"In a little hot water?" Grimes said.

"Something like that. More like a lot of hot water."

He chuckled. "Takes more than some hot water to soften up this old piece of leather. I've had to do some damage control, but I'm managing."

"Glad to hear it."

"Managing better than some, I should say," Grimes said.

"You mean Sam," Julia said, and an odd little sensation fluttered up from around her solar plexus.

"I do. I'm worried about him. And there aren't a whole lot of people around here I can confess that to right now."

"So I'm guessing there was more to it all than Sam being a 'person of interest' in a case."

"I heard about that line of BS," Grimes scoffed. "Yeah, there's more to it."

"How much more?" Julia asked, not sure she wanted to hear the answer. Sky shoved his head under her hand. She rubbed absently at his ears.

Grimes sighed. "A few decades more. Fair to say there's bad blood between those two."

Julia made a soft sound of agreement. "His father sounds like a piece of work."

"The thing is, Sam always had a little spirit in him. A little push-back. Now ... " Grimes trailed off. "He's different. I'd say he seems ... defeated."

"What's happening?"

There was a long pause. Long enough that Julia wondered if the call had dropped. "Grimes? What's—"

"Magnus put Sam on Empire's Board of Directors."

Julia gaped. "He did *what?*"

"It's not a real position. Sam doesn't have any power there. Magnus just put him somewhere he could keep an eye on Sam."

"What's Sam doing, then?"

"Hell if I know. Mainly I think he's trying to keep from going stir-crazy. The kid's bored. He tries to pretend he's not for my benefit, but Sam's never been able to put one over on me. I've known that boy since before he was born."

Julia smiled fondly. "He's lucky to have you on his side over there."

"For all the good it's doing him. I'm not Magnus's favorite person either these days."

"It's weird, though, isn't it? He barely tolerates his son. Why the big push to have him involved in the family business?"

"And Sam's hardly involved. I agree it doesn't make a lick of sense. Tell you the truth, it makes me think Magnus is up to something."

Julia looked up at the moon through the greenhouse panels. A spider sat in a web high above her. "What kind of 'something'?"

"I can't say I'm sure, but something sure as hell's trying to worm its way to the surface."

She tipped her head back as the moon came out from behind a cloud, illuminating the panes of glass. Her gaze went again to the spider in its web; in the moonlight she spied the spider and its web again but now she saw one or two tightly wrapped parcels snagged in the silk.

Dammit, Sam. What have you fallen into?

26

Unknown Location

This time, he would make no mistakes. He had heard the commands of his master loud and clear, and the still-weeping wounds on his back reminded him of his failures with every slight movement.

Uzziel watched her from a distance, measuring the patterns of her life, determining where best he could strike, could cut, could capture. The task was not an easy one; she vanished for long periods. But even the canniest prey needed to surface every now and again, if only for air and sustenance.

The hour had not yet come to put his plan into action. But when it did, he would be ready. He would strike swift and silent, alone. Antarctica had taught him that much. Others were a liability. Others were variables beyond his control.

And his master had been firm.

No mistakes.

No errors.

Uzziel bowed his head and curled his shoulders, breaking more of the scabs beneath his clothing. The pain seared through him, cleansing and clarifying.

No failure.

27

Light Hall, Irving, Texas

Jack Henley looked at the sea of young faces in front of her. She was always surprised at how quickly and easily a team of some of the brightest, hardest working supporters and rabble rousers could be assembled when they felt impassioned and were paid well. Mostly paid well.

The six months from when she and Tommy Jones had first proposed the idea of Magnus Sawyer hitting the campaign trail pitching the idea of natural gas as a solution to the climate crisis, until today, had seemed a lifetime ago, yet here they were in a rented Dallas, Texas auditorium waiting for Magnus Sawyer's keynote address. The team had spared no expense: television cameras, bright lights, a handful of photographers, and hiring the most sought after speech writer in the country, Aaron Siegel.

"Thanks to all of you for coming out today to support Mr. Sawyer," said Jack. The crowd had been well groomed. They clapped loudly and even a few added hoots and whistles.

“Now, I have some exciting news,” said Jack. “Mr. Sawyer has agreed to give his first major speech this afternoon!” The room lit up with excitement. Her team had done a good job of getting the right people with the right energy to bolster Magnus's confidence. She waited for the excitement to die down, then glanced sideways to make sure Magnus stood at the ready behind the curtain.

“Ladies and gentlemen, members of the press, it is my great honor to introduce you to the CEO of Empire Oil, Magnus E. Sawyer.”

Magnus broke a big, practiced smile as he approached the podium. He put his hands up to quiet the crowd, remembered to pull the smile from his face, offering his most dignified expression, then glanced at the sea of faces. “Thank you all for coming out today.”

Magnus adjusted his feet, composed himself, and looked again at the crowd through the teleprompter glass as it began to scroll the words of Aaron Siegel.

“Good evening. I am here tonight to launch my campaign to Bring Back America.

“In 1776, we fought to gain our independence from the chains of foreign interests, and we won."

Magnus had practiced his most determined face in the mirror.

"America was born on that date as an independent God-fearing nation of the people and for the people. We began as a sovereign nation of merchants and farmers, a shining beacon the world would come to admire. Today we are at a crossroads, a turning point in our history where once again, we find ourselves trapped in the bondage of debt and dependence on others. Our nation’s light now flickers."

He waited for the pause indicated on the teleprompter screen.

“Our national debt is approaching 35 trillion dollars." He paused again and the teleprompter waited for his off script remarks. "That's trillion with a T!" He scanned the crowd’s many faces.

"We depend on others to finance this debt, more so every year. America has never been weaker. Our nation drifts from one crisis to the next, unsure of where to go and what to do. We bicker over trivial issues and avoid the tough decisions—decisions like what to do about global warming, the national debt, high taxes, and returning God to our nation. Our future is at risk."

He waited for the applause to quiet.

"Families struggle to make ends meet despite working as hard as they can. Washington's answer? Same as always: increase taxes and borrow even more. Am I right?" He shook his head agreeing with the crowd. "Them politicians pump up entitlements when what we Americans want is greater economic opportunity, not a handout." He stole a sideways glance at Jack's off stage thumbs up.

Magnus turned back to the crowd with a stern face.

"Over the last decade, we've accepted our weakened position. Them Washington politicians tell us they are doing their best in the face of problems—that we should be happy and learn to live with less while the size of government is greater than at any time in the past. Does any of that seem right to y'all?"

The chorus of boos reverberated in the room.

"No, 'course not." He jabbed his index finger at the audience. "It's time for change. America is still the greatest nation on earth. It's our duty to lead the world and regain what has always been rightfully ours. It is time to Bring Back America!"

The crowd cheered.

"Today we face an erosion of power and a failure of leadership unprecedented in American history. The federal government has overspent and over-regulated. Other nations hold our country's capital and energy needs hostage. We are asked by our own leaders to use less energy; to conserve, to turn a blind eye to our needs as a country. If we follow the course them Washington boys have laid out for us, the day will come when the wheels of industry will fall off the wagon and our country's lights will dim."

He waited for quiet. "You ready for that to happen?"

A roar from the crowd answered his question.

"Me neither! It's time for us to return to the principles on which our great nation was founded: independence, fiscal responsibility, God, and the moral fiber to stand as a sovereign nation. In the immortal words of Thomas Jefferson, 'The purpose of government is to enable the people of a nation to live in safety and happiness. Government exists for the interests of the governed, not for the governors."

This was the loudest applause he had yet received.

"America may be the greatest experiment on Earth, but we have lost our footing as the symbol of prosperity. It doesn't have to be that way. America can pull itself up from the darkness." He raised his hands above his head and pointed to the heavens "To strengthen our nation, we must work to slow climate change, reduce our dependence on foreign oil, get our nation switched over from coal and oil to clean natural gas, bring God back into our communities, and return the power taken from us back home."

The roar from the crowd was almost too much.

"We've made great strides in domestic energy production over the last decade, but it's time we stop paying ransom to those big oil companies that are heating the planet and sucking our wallets dry."

The teleprompter ticked off the time he should wait before speaking again.

"I'll be honest with ya' all. I'm a Texas oil man. Been so all my life. I was raised both a Christian and an oil man. My daddy was an oil man and his daddy too. But times are different now. We have a crisis on our hands and it's time we changed. Changed from burning coal and oil to burning clean natural gas."

The crowd was a mix of cheers and boos.

"Now, I know. Some of you'd rather just shut off the fossil fuel spigot tomorrow but that ain't responsible. Look. We have a big country here. Most powerful in the world, and I'm not going to propose anything that slows us down or harms us. Natural gas is twice as clean as coal and oil. Let's make it step one of a future of fixing climate change."

The applause was greater now.

"Ya with me?" He bellowed out to the crowd as the teleprompter waited for him to return to the script. "We can do this, and I'm going to tell you how."

The teleprompter began its roll again.

“In the middle of our great country lies the largest reserve of natural gas in the world. It's called the Green River Formation. It contains more energy than all the oil in the Mideast, Russia, Canada, and South America combined. It contains more energy than the world has ever used since the industrial revolution.

“Extracting the energy will not be easy, yet we have had the means to do so for years. The Green River Formation is America's greatest treasure and yet its best kept secret. Most Americans have never heard of it, and I believe I know why."

He paused until the crowd quieted.

"Some in Washington seek to hide this truth from Americans, putting profits before our nation's welfare. They take the easy road that puts our nation at risk. As CEO of Empire Oil, I will open these rich energy fields in an environmentally clean and safe way and bring America back to its rightful position as the healthiest nation on Earth. By returning America to energy independence and economic health we can rebuild our nation's infrastructure, remove the threat posed by foreign oil, restore American jobs and pride, bring God back into our nation and help end global warming. We will regain what we lost and be freed from the shackles of foreign oil and debt.

“An independent nation is a prosperous nation. One of my heroes, Ronald Reagan said, 'A nation that is growing and thriving is one which can solve its problems. We must offer progress instead of stagnation, truth instead of promises, hope and faith instead of defeatism and despair. Then we'll make decisions that'll restore confidence in our way of life and release that energy of the American spirit.”

He didn't have to watch the teleprompter any longer. He could sense when it was right to speak again.

“Help me restore America's leadership in the world. Together, we can and will bring America back again to its rightful place on earth, that of the greatest nation under God. Thank you, and may God bless America.”

Magnus stood triumphant on the podium, feeling invincible, his face lit bright by the camera's flashing. The room was filled with the deafening roar of approval.

"I guess they liked it," he said to Jack.

Jack stopped and turned to Magnus. "Liked it, Mr. Sawyer? Are you kidding me? They loved it."

28

Dallas, Texas

Julia woke to her cell phone vibrating insistently on her bedside table. She blinked groggily, trying to clear the cobwebs from her head as she groped around for the sleek little rectangle demanding her attention. She saw the time of day and the name of her caller at precisely the same moment.

"H'lo?" she muttered, wondering why on Earth Betty Faulkner would be phoning her at a quarter to five in the morning.

"Rise and shine, Dr. Bassi. There's a little party down in linguistics you'll want to join."

Julia sat up and pushed a hand through her hair. "What?" she asked, snapping on the bedside lamp. Sky lifted his head from the foot of her bed and regarded her sleepily—and maybe a little annoyed.

"Trust me on this one, just get your rear out of bed and come down here. Oh—and don't worry about the coffee. We've got a steady stream of it going right now."

"Yeah," Julia replied, groggily despite her best efforts, "sounds like it."

"You'll be glad you did," Betty replied, before closing the connection.

Julia pushed back the covers and dressed hastily, pulling on a sweatshirt over the T-shirt she'd been sleeping in and yanking on a pair of sweatpants she snagged from a pile of clean-but-unfolded laundry. She shoved her feet into her slippers and opened the door, glancing at Sky over her shoulder.

"You want to come along? I don't blame you if you'd rather not."

Sky pushed to his feet, stretched elaborately, and hopped off the bed. He joined her at the door and gave Julia's hand a brief lick.

"I appreciate the company, buddy," she said, and the two started for the linguistics division.

Of all the things Julia was prepared to find, it wasn't four of the most brilliant individuals she'd met in recent memory sitting around a table surrounded by pizza boxes, soda cans, and paper coffee cups. Betty, Harry, James, and Dai-Lu sat amid the carnage, looking strangely pleased.

Julia took a seat and two slices of cold pizza, one for Sky and the other she started munching on.

"Ok, you got me and Sky out of bed, what's going on?"

Harry gave her an apologetic smile. "I came down here to pick Betty's brain about the latest round of context-based translations. James was already here trying to solve a different issue; anyway, we all got to talking and before I knew it, the conversation had moved to mythology."

"Talking ... about mythology?" Julia asked, smothering a yawn.

"Norse mythology, to be precise," Betty said as James helped himself to a piece of cold pizza. He was unusually disheveled—or perhaps not so unusually, if he'd been up all night.

Dai-Lu got up and came back with a fresh cup of hot coffee, which she pressed into Julia's hand. "That should help."

"Thank you." Julia took a sip. It was strong enough to ease away some of her lingering sleepiness. "Are you telling me you all just started talking about ... Norse mythology? Out of the blue?"

"Not entirely out of the blue," James replied.

"Have you ever heard of the term, Ragnarök?" asked Harry.

Julia stared at them all and shook her head. "I'm familiar with the term, but *my* original major was pre-med, so you'll have to forgive me for not knowing more than that."

"Ragnarök," Harry explained, "is essentially the end of the world, according to Norse mythology."

"The term first appeared in the thirteenth century," James said, "in a series of anonymous poems."

Harry shook her head. "No, it was the tenth, but the text in question was technically Icelandic, which is a detail that doesn't really matter given our purposes. A poem, *Völuspá*. The thirteenth century text shows similarities to the earlier Icelandic one."

"Without getting too technical," Betty said, "the word *Ragnarök* basically translates to 'Twilight of the Gods.' Or, if you want the more cheerful translation, 'Doom of the Gods.'" She paused. "It's such a decisive end, even the gods are powerless to stop it."

That woke her up. Julia took another bite of pizza. "All right. What's been written about the Norse version of the end of days?"

"Nothing good," Harry answered. "Catastrophic natural disasters, mostly. The sun goes dark. The stars vanish. Fires and floods ravage the land until nothing is left, at which point the world is reborn, fertile and green."

"And not just *floods*," Dai-Lu said, pointedly. "The whole world is supposed to disappear into the sea."

"Sound familiar?" Harry asked.

Julia nodded slowly. "A little too familiar."

"Now," Betty interjected, "the interesting part. The Norse goddess Frigg is frequently associated with, among other things, motherhood and prophecy. She is also said to live in Fensalir, commonly believed to be a wet, boggy locale."

"Keep that in mind," Harry said as Julia fed Sky another chunk of pizza crust under the table.

"In the Lofoten archipelago," James said, "there is an obscure bit of local legend regarding Frigg, specifically. It's said that there is a shrine deep beneath the waters near the town of Reine where Frigg spirited away expecting mothers to protect them from dangerous trolls. There are variations of the story here and there—some say she protected young mothers and small children in her shrine, some legends suggest she did the same for whole families."

Julia nodded slowly, all the pieces gradually coming together and forming an almost coherent picture. "Aha. And, of course, what do you need to protect when the end of the world comes?"

Harry met her eyes. "The ones who will rebuild in the aftermath. It goes beyond lore; it's a biological imperative. Survival."

"In case of Ragnarök, break glass," Dai-Lu said. "Or, in this case, summon goddess."

29

Highland Park, Texas

Lunches that turned into dinner meetings with Tommy and Jack had become a staple of Magnus's life. That, and his twice weekly speeches kept him on the move. Once every couple of weeks, he'd get the summons from Tommy. Dutifully, he'd show up, nod along, reassure Tommy that his investment was a sure thing, and pay for a ridiculously expensive meal that Tommy could've sprung for with the money in his pockets.

"Magnus," said Tommy, running his fingers through his slicked-back hair before resting them on a stomach already full of steak and foie gras on Magnus's dime. "I want to put on a celebration. With you givin' speeches and riling everyone up, and Jack's support getting folks thinking it might be ok, what we're doin', it's time we ramped up the idea of Thermal Fracking. This well's gonna change the world. Hell, we are going to change the world. We want everyone to know it."

Magnus nodded and signaled the waiter for another whiskey. He already knew this was a meal where he'd want the bar to keep them coming. "I'm not disagreeing, but—"

Tommy chuckled. "But you're disagreeing. You going squirrelly on me, Sawyer? You want all the limelight for yourself? You don't think this is something worth celebrating?"

"It's the protesters. They want us to stop using fossil fuels and switch over to solar. They say natural gas isn't a solution but rather part of the problem. Environmentalists. I am getting boos for my speeches. They've turned on me, Tommy. A party is only going to add fuel to their fire. I don't think it's a good idea."

"And I want a harem of blondes who'll follow my every command," said Tommy. "We don't always get what we want."

Jack shook her head, but Magnus didn't miss the disgusted scowl she shot Tommy's way. "They're just idealists."

Magnus lowered his eyes to the plate and slowly sliced off a blood-red piece of meat. "I've gotten death threats."

Tommy pushed himself away from the table. "You don't pay any attention to those crazies, Magnus. You sure as shit don't let 'em win. It's gas. Clean natural gas, and don't you forget it."

Jack smiled and placed her hand gently on Magnus's forearm. "I think what Tommy's trying to say is that, with the right spin, we can turn the attention to our advantage. Just think of all the excitement your Bring Back America campaign had when we first launched it. We can get it back, I promise you. Just hang in there Magnus."

Whenever Jack spoke, Magnus couldn't help but believe her. Tommy, he was always too tense, too over-the-top. Jack knew her game. Spoke Magnus's language. She lowered her voice as if sharing a secret. "Protesters get energized by being on one side of an issue. Sometimes they get a bit carried away. But we're on the right track. We're on the right side of history. We're not destroying the planet; we're weaning the most powerful nation on Earth off coal and oil. We're *saving* them, Magnus. They'll see that in time. And then they'll be singing your praises instead of protesting your work. You see?"

Magnus downed his drink as soon as the waiter set it down and gestured for another.

"Magnus," said Tommy, retaking his seat. "You a huntin' man?"

Magnus blinked, startled. "I hunt."

"Good," Tommy said, looking at his watch. "Meet me at my plane in an hour. We're headin' to Colorado for a little elk shoot. Just you and me, Magnus. We'll work out the details of this event, man to man."

"Sure," said Magnus in a hoarse whisper. "Just you and me. Man to man."

30

Vail, Colorado

Magnus arose at dawn, rubbed his swollen blue eyes, drank a glass of water, and headed to the hotel bathroom for Tylenol. A few minutes later he lurched downstairs to meet Tommy Jones, and their hunting guide. His head was still reeling from the lunch-turned-dinner the day before. The last thing he wanted to do was spend the day swaying on the back of a horse, but maybe time alone with Tommy would give him the chance to set the record straight, remind Tommy that once those bills were paid, Magnus would be back on top.

And Tommy? Well. Tommy's services would no longer be required. Not that Magnus planned to spend much time on that topic. Hell, sometimes Tommy talked like *he* owned Empire, when all he'd done was provide a seed loan at an astronomical interest rate.

They drove to a trailhead in Minturn Magnus wasn't familiar with. Saddled horses already waited for them. Magnus mounted a chestnut mare, Tommy an appaloosa. The group plodded up a narrow snow crusted gully alongside a frozen stream that meandered through an aspen grove. Magnus buttoned the top latch on his jacket and pulled his knit cap over his ears. After an hour, they stopped and dismounted for lunch in a quiet snowfield. Two of the guide's men, following with the pack horse, rushed over to help Tommy and Magnus off their mounts.

The packers set out portable propane heaters and pointed them at a lunch spread on a folding table. They opened cans of beer, and motioned for everyone to sit next to one of the heaters. As they ate, one of the packers spotted something in the brush and motioned for quiet. He crept past the table, pulled his rifle from its scabbard, and checked to make sure it was loaded. Tommy gulped the last of his beer and dropped his sandwich. He nudged Magnus to follow. The packer put his finger to his lips. They peered through thick frozen brush at a large cow elk who had broken through the ice of a small pond and was drinking from the cold water.

Excited, Tommy tapped the young packer's shoulder. "Give me the gun," he whispered, his voice muffled by the sound of the creek. "I can get a clean shot." The man looked at him for several seconds.

Magnus understood the hesitation; taking an animal down while it was drinking, oblivious to danger, wasn't sporting. A real hunter, a good hunter, didn't need to resort to that kind of cowardice.

Reluctantly, the packer handed over the rifle. Tommy disengaged the safety without a sound, raised the stock to his shoulder and pulled the trigger. Missed. The animal bolted at the crack of the shot. Tommy fired in rapid succession, and one round struck the fleeing cow's back. She fell a hundred yards away, struggling to rise onto her front legs.

Magnus's ears rang with the reverberation of the shots. He lingered a little behind as Tommy and the packer rushed to where the cow was floundering on the snowy ground. Tommy, still grasping the rifle, walked across the frozen stream and stood looking at the wounded cow. She was bleeding badly but still struggling to escape, bellowing with pain.

Looking away from the cow, Magnus happened to glimpse

Tommy's face. It was shining with perspiration and a certain gleefulness that made goosepimples rise on Magnus's arms. *It's almost like he's enjoying watching her suffer.*

The packer reached out a hand to Tommy. "Sir, give me the rifle. I'm going to put her down."

Tommy pull the rifle close and glared at the young man. "The hell you will. This is my kill. If there's any more shooting to be done, I'll be the one pulling the trigger."

The guide backed away. "Okay, okay. But ... sir, she's suffering. You gotta put her down. Now." The elk stopped struggling and lay panting in the snow, her dark brown eyes wide.

"No one's going to shoot her. She's mine, and I intend to enjoy her till it's finished." Tommy turned and gazed down at the animal, a feral smile on his face.

Magnus, swallowing hard, moved next to him. "Tommy, this ain't right. Put the thing out of its misery and let's finish lunch. This ain't the way we Texans handle things."

Tommy directed his smile at Magnus. "No, Magnus, it's not." He leaned in close and whispered, "I just want to make sure we both understand who's runnin' the show here. 'Cause I think maybe you forgot. I think all that attention you get at them rallies is getting to your head. I think you might have forgotten just who they are really cheering for. Tell me, Magnus. Who is it they are really cheering for?"

Magnus cleared his throat. The dying gasps of the elk rang in his ears. "You are."

"There's a time to be born, a time to die ... and a time to kill. *I* get to decide who does what. No one's gettin' in my way, Magnus. Not you. Not Jack Henley. Not a bunch of pussy protesters. You're with me or against me. There's no in between, Magnus."

Tommy stared at Magnus for another endless moment before turning toward the cow elk, his face still shone with an eerie pleasure. The elk's thrashing increased the closer Tommy got. Tommy stooped to look right into the cow's eyes. The cow gave a series of short, gasping grunts. Magnus closed his eyes as a shot shattered the silence of the aspen grove and echoed off the valley walls.

The sound had only just disappeared when Tommy's was at Magnus's side once again. He looped his arm through Magnus's and said cheerfully, "Now wasn't that exciting? Worked up quite an appetite. Come on, Magnus. We've got a party to plan, don't we?" Tommy grinned. "Let's blow this one out of the water."

31

Leknes, Norway

Leknes Regional Airport was compact and practical: a single runway and a no-frills terminal, its tarmac roughly the size of a football field.

Once off the plane, Julia huddled down in her parka, gloved hands tucked in her pockets while James tucked his scarf more firmly into his coat. Sky clambered down the plane's narrow steps, legs stretching into a run—his first since the flight began.

"A model passenger, all things considered," James said, nodding at Sky as he ran in wide circles before relieving himself on a patch of grass.

Julia smiled but did not mention that this was hardly Sky's first time traveling long-distance. "He sure is."

The two of them had flown to Norway by private jet to sidestep the usual complications of bringing dogs into the country; this method of travel also allowed them to travel ... if not completely unnoticed, then at least *less* noticed. They'd even left their cell phones behind, at Harry's insistence. Passports were checked first in Germany, but once inside the EU, they managed the flight to Norway without gathering more attention.

James and Julia picked up their pace, boots crunching as they walked briskly across the tarmac toward the terminal. The sliding doors opened, enveloping them in a gust of warmer air; they retrieved their luggage and made their way toward the loaner vehicle Harry had arranged for them.

"Shall I drive?" James offered.

"Be my guest," Julia replied. "I'll navigate. Let's see if we can reach Reine before sunset."

James turned the key and the Land Rover's diesel engine roared to life, its grumble drowning out the soft pelt of rain that had started to freckle the windshield.

As they drove along Lofoten's narrow roads, there was no shortage of natural beauty. On one side, vast blue fjords stretched endlessly, while on the other, towering granite walls, carved over millennia by glaciers, erupted from the water. The rain varied in intensity, sometimes little more than in intermittent mist, while other times a full downpour, pelting the vehicle's roof.

"Do you mind if I ask you something?"

Julia shrugged. "It'll be a long, boring ride if we don't talk. What's up?"

"What . . . " James's hesitation, his body language, caught Julia's attention more than his words. "What happened in Antarctica?" He shook his head. "I know what Harry communicated to us, but . . . "

"But you'd like to hear it straight from the horse's mouth."

"Yes."

Julia nodded slowly. "Well. The whole reason we went in the first place was because Karl Satsky had been abducted."

"By . . . Uzziel, was it?" James asked. "His group, the Sons of Nephilim."

"Right. And . . . honestly, I know it sounds like I'm describing some cheesy action flick, but . . . it was a trap. The whole thing was a trap. We drilled a hole half a mile deep into the ice sheet—at gunpoint. And then we lowered Sam and Dr. Satsky down into it. Also at gunpoint."

"Without knowing whether any of you would survive?" he asked.

Julia nodded. "He found it, though. The pyramid, obviously, or we wouldn't be here." She told him the rest, the destruction of the pyramid, the deaths of Grimes's friends and coworkers—emotion further tightened her throat as she tried to give Satsky dignity in the retelling of his death.

Silence stretched between them so thick it wrapped around them, filling every crevice of the car.

"At least," Julia said, taking a deep breath. "At least here we have a fighting chance, right?"

"Indeed," James replied, nodding slowly. "And we won't waste it."

Ninety minutes into their trip, they came upon the village of Reine, cheerful red rorbuer along the coast, casting nearly perfect reflections in the crystalline water. Behind it stood Reinebringen Mountain, perfectly snowcapped. The sun had not yet set, throwing a golden cast over the village.

James parked and they unloaded their luggage, making their way to their assigned cabins. Julia unlocked the door to hers and stepped inside; it was already blissfully warm, thanks to a wood stove in the front sitting area. Sky wagged his tail and made a beeline for the braided rug in front of the stove. He turned in a circle and lay down.

"Just going to embrace that stereotype, huh Sky?" Julia asked as she shrugged out of her coat and pulled off her boots.

The cabin itself was rustic and cozy. Beautifully patterned area rugs covered the wood floors in the sitting room, which featured two armchairs and a small sofa. The kitchen was well-appointed, and someone—the same someone who'd gotten the wood stove going—had left the kitchen stocked with groceries for them. On the kitchen table she found a map of the terrain. At the far end of the cabin was the bedroom, an inviting double bed covered in a vivid woolen coverlet. She went next door to James's cabin and knocked; he opened the door, an electric kettle already in hand.

"It's been a long day," Julia said. "Let's get some shut eye and venture out tomorrow, first thing."

"Agreed," he said. "Besides, it will be dark soon. Better if we rest and start fresh in the morning."

Julia went back to her cabin and cobbled together a meal from the provisions left for her in the kitchen. Whoever had done the shopping had included a bag of dog food for Sky, which he devoured with relish. After dinner, Julia curled up on the little sofa in front of the wood stove, the satellite phone—a gift from Harry—in her hand.

Check in with me once a day. I want to know your progress, but I also want to know if you hit any snags.

Julia dialed and waited as the line rang.

"Julia!" Harry answered. "How's Norway?"

"A little chilly, compared to Texas, but nothing I can't handle."

"I have some intel for you—a colleague of mine in Oslo says you won't find a better guide in Reine than Lars Nilsen.

"Lars Nilsen," Julia repeated, writing down the name. "Got it."

32

Reine Village, Lofoten archipelago

Julia slept solidly, waking well before the sun rose. Momentarily disoriented, she checked her watch—it was 7:00 AM, two hours before sunrise. She washed and dressed before taking Sky out for a brief walk. By the time she returned, her stomach was growling. She found brown bread, cheese, and locally cured salmon.

"I can definitely put something together with all this," she said.

After eating, Julia went next door to collect James and they ventured into the village, Sky trotting happily alongside Julia. After a few twists and a couple of wrong turns, they came upon their destination: Lars Nilsen: Guided Fishing Expeditions.

Inside, the shop was warm, smelling like a curious blend of sea salt and strong coffee. Behind the counter stood Lars: tall and broad, his skin weathered by the elements, dark hair streaked liberally with silver. Sharp blue eyes crinkled at the corners when he smiled as they entered.

"Good morning!" Lars said, greeting them both with a booming voice. "How can I help you?"

Julia and James approached the counter, introducing themselves, as Sky gave the shop a cursory sniff before settling at Julia's side.

"My colleague and I require a guide with a thorough knowledge of local lore," Julia said.

Lars cocked his head to one side. "I am a fishing guide, not a tour guide."

"Understood," said Julia, "however, we have been told you have certain knowledge that might be valuable to us."

Lars stood with arms folded.

"Do you know anything about a local shrine to Frigg?" James asked.

Lars shook his head at that. "You will find many shrines to many of our old gods."

Julia exchanged a brief glance with James. "Do you know anything about an underwater shrine to Frigg?"

That made Lars stop. "What did you say?"

Julia swallowed; her mouth had gone suddenly dry. "A shrine. A *hof?* To Frigg. But ... underwater. Or near water?"

"According to the legend," James said, "Frigg protected mothers and children from wandering troll tribes."

Slowly, Lars nodded. "There are stories about Frigg, yes. Some, not many, about what you ask."

"What kinds of stories?" James asked. "Is there truly such a location?"

"There is a man I knew once. He ... " Lars hesitated. "He and his wife asked another guide about that site. That guide sent them to me." He smiled fondly, but the smile was tinged with sadness. "They loved to travel together, to find locations boasting obscure bits of legend and myth."

"Tried to find it?" James echoed. "Were they not successful?"

"His wife disappeared," Lars said. "They found nothing of her." He paused, shaking his head. "Gale was heartbroken. Nora was pregnant. With their first. Losing his wife ... broke him."

Julia went perfectly still when she heard those words. "She ... vanished?"

Lars nodded. "I do not think he will speak with you. I'm not sure he would speak to me—I have not seen him in years. Not since ... not since then. He's become a recluse."

"Can you take us there to see if we can find him?" asked James.

"There is nothing to see. I told you, he's a recluse now."

"It's important," said Julia. "For us, there is nothing more important. It is why we travelled thousands of miles. Please?"

Lars sighed. "If you insist. But you will come back empty handed. This I promise."

"We accept the risk."

Lars bit his lower lip before speaking. "I will ferry you to Frigg's shrine in three days. I cannot do it sooner—I'm sorry."

"I understand," said Julia. "Three days—we can make that work."

"There may be more of us by then," said James. "Will there be room on the boat for three or four more?"

Lars smiled. "You clearly have not seen my boat. There's plenty of room. Come by the shop early tomorrow and I'll show you the boat and my maps of the area."

33

Dallas, Texas

Screw heart disease, diabetes, or car accidents. Sam was going to die of boredom. He could see it now. One of these days, at one of these godawful, endless parties, he was going to take yet another sip of godawful, tepid champagne and drop dead.

Hell, he didn't even know what this party was *for.* He vaguely recognized some of the milling faces, all grinning as much as their Botox would allow, but no matter how much small talk he eavesdropped on, he couldn't figure out if this was some kind of awards night, fundraiser, benefit, or something else entirely.

The champagne didn't improve after the first glass, which was a shame. Sam glanced at his watch, dismayed to realize only half an hour had passed since his arrival. No chance of escape for hours yet.

A woman whose natural beauty, if she'd ever had it, had long since been carved away and replaced with the blandness of plastic surgeon's work swayed up to him. Her sequined gown shimmered in the golden light as she laid a manicured hand on his arm. Even standing this close to her, he couldn't begin to guess her age. She wore too much perfume and giggled at nothing in a way that told him she'd already imbibed too much of the free alcohol. "So," she simpered, fluttering her obviously fake eyelashes. "You're the Sawyer boy. My, my."

He fought back the grimace that ached to crease his face. "You have me at a disadvantage, ma'am."

Again, she giggled. "And so polite!"

So bored. So very bored.

The grip on his arm tightened. "Your mama and I were thick as thieves, back in the day."

Sam blinked and couldn't mask his astonishment quickly enough. Even at the outside, he hadn't thought her old enough to be his mother. The woman clearly followed this line of thought because she leaned in a whispered conspiratorially, "Why, yes. I do have the *very* best surgeon in town. I take that look of yours as a compliment, young man. Now, you wouldn't remember me, of course. Your daddy ran off all your mama's friends when she up and left him. But I changed your diaper more than once, I'll have you know."

Hell is a party where an older woman who looks half her age talks about changing my diapers, Sam thought. *And here I always wondered what Satan might have cooked up for me.*

He cleared his throat. "I—sorry, ma'am. Your name escapes me."

She lifted one bare shoulder in a shrug that looked oddly girlish. The pressure of her hand on his arm increased, nudging him toward the corner of the room, even though her expression never changed.

And the giggle was really starting to freak him out.

Without releasing his arm, she reached for a fresh flute of champagne. The hotel ballroom didn't exactly have privacy, but she'd managed to guide him into a quieter corner. He glanced over her shoulder at the crowd, wondering what it was all for, but the sharp way she cleared her throat brought his attention back to her in an instant.

With none of her earlier fawning, she said quietly, "I was also your mother's divorce lawyer, Samuel."

The change in her tone brought his attention fully back to her. Her body language still said 'unrepentant flirt' but the expression on her face was anything but flirtatious. She took a fake sip of alcohol, giggled again, and said, "What are you doing here?"

Sam had the urge to pinch himself to make sure he wasn't dreaming. "They tell me where to go, and I go. They say jump, I ask how high."

"They?"

"The Board. My father. The great Empire Oil. When the marching orders come in, I march."

She rolled her eyes. "Thought you had more of Mary-Beth's fire in you than that."

Sam pulled his arm from beneath her hand and scowled. "Look, lady, I don't know you, and I barely knew my mom. I definitely didn't know her long enough or well enough to pick up her damn personality or habits. She made sure of that."

The woman shook her head slowly, eyes widening. "So you don't know a damn thing about any of it, then." She uttered a low, disbelieving whistle. "Real piece of work, your daddy."

"Tell me something I don't know."

"Why else would I be here now?" she asked. "This ... fracking venture. How much do you know about it?"

"As little as I could possibly get away with," Sam replied. "Just being here makes me sick enough as it is."

"Do you know how your daddy's paying for it?"

Sam frowned. "What's that supposed to mean?"

"Five months ago, Empire was on the brink of collapse. Debt collectors rumbling. Other companies hovering like vultures over a deer about to get hit by a car."

Sam shook his head. "It couldn't have been that bad."

She raised her meticulously plucked eyebrows. "No? Your daddy stopped taking calls, even from his own investors. Even from his own Board. He was desperate, Samuel. Desperate like a man who knows he's drowning and the only other creatures in the water with him are sharks."

All trace of the giggling idiot had vanished, replaced by deadly seriousness. Sam leaned in. She said, "Then, wonder of wonders, the prodigal son returns, and Daddy Sawyer immediately jumps on the fracking bandwagon to the tune of at least twenty million dollars. Where *did* he find that cold, hard cash? Sure as shit wasn't in *his* bank account. And I guarantee it wasn't in Empire's either."

Sam chuckled uncomfortably. "If you're suggesting that *I* bankrolled him, you have no idea how much academics make."

"Oh, I know it wasn't your account, either." She raised her eyes and stared at him, unflinching. "At least, none of the ones you know about."

"I'm sor—"

She continued on blithely, as if he hadn't interrupted her. "It's just, when Magnus ran your mama outta town—and he did, make no mistake—I got a real good look at the paperwork. And then I hear that his kid, the same kid who went off to study climate science, is suddenly back at Empire. I found myself wondering why that might be. Why the kid who got out might've been sucked back in." She turned a blinding smile his way. "And so I came to a few of these shindigs. And every time I saw the kid, he was sullen. Sad. Obviously not enjoying himself."

"It's not—"

"Now, client privilege means I gotta watch my tongue. I'm not saying Mary-Beth made the choice I might have done in her place, but I can tell you this much—she knew what she was worth. And she'd be pissed as hell if she thought the bastard who fought her on every nickel was, say, stealing from his own kid's inheritance after everything he stole from her."

Sam's jaw dropped. He reached for words but found only sputtering noises. The woman reached out and patted him lightly on the cheek. "You're a good boy, Samuel. I can see it. You're nothing like *him.* For your sake—and maybe a little for your mama's—you should do some digging. Your Grandpa Henry really was so *thrilled* when you were born."

She giggled, and the mask of bubbly, brainless socialite slid down over her features once again. Before Sam could do more than gasp out the word "Wait," she'd disappeared into the crowd again.

I didn't even get her name.

And yet. Something about her words was like the splash of cold water he used to wake himself up in the morning. For months, his father had been giving him bullshit tasks and sending him to bullshit parties. For months, Sam had felt like his brain was slowly leaking out his ear, to be replaced with bad champagne, the stench of oil, and the certainty that he'd lost access to the only life that had ever truly excited him.

But now?

Now, he had a problem to solve. A hypothesis to prove or disprove.

Sam put down the glass of too-warm wine and smiled. Then he turned his back on the stupid party full of people he never wanted to see again. He didn't look at the time; the time for caring about that was over.

He grinned.

Research had always been his favorite part.

34

Reine Village, Lofoten archipelago

Julia knocked on James's door just before seven. She'd called Harry to check in after getting off the phone with Lars the night before; but, afterward, when she went to James's cabin to tell him they had an early morning, her knocks went unanswered.

And they were still going unanswered.

It's nothing, she told herself. He might've been in the shower last night. Or he might've fallen asleep. Or he could be in the shower *now.* There were plenty of reasonable explanations.

I'll try again when I come back. It's still early—he could be asleep.

Julia and Sky started for Lars's shop—sunrise was over two hours away, but the little village was well lit and Julia had an easier time finding the place this time around.

The coffee aroma was stronger this morning than yesterday—probably because the man in question had just finished brewing a fresh pot.

"You are admirably early," he said. "No companion?"

"It's just me and Sky this morning," Julia replied. "I suspect my colleague is still asleep."

Together they pored over maps and Lars showed her their location as well as his planned route to get there. "Kjerkfjorden Caves," he said, stabbing the map with a thick index finger. "It will be a long journey. You should bring provisions."

"What about camping supplies?"

"A good idea, if you have them handy."

"Not exactly, but I'll advise the others of our party to pack accordingly."

Just then the door opened with surprising force, rebounding off the wall of the shop. Julia looked up, startled—and was doubly startled to see a man whose entire body took up the doorway. He was older than Lars and three times as weathered. He wore a battered leather jacket and a deep green knitted cap over his head; tufts of silver hair stuck out below his ears and at his temples.

"Lars," the old man grumbled. His voice was rough and deep. Julia thought for a moment it was the type of voice you needed to be heard above crashing waves.

"Arnar," Lars said, waving the older man in. "Here's someone I want you to meet."

"The fool who wants to be taken to the *hof*," Arnar said, glowering at Julia before turning his ire back to Lars. "Are you mad or just stupid?"

Lars sighed and looked at Julia. "Arnar has agreed—though his demeanor doesn't show it—to sail with us."

"It's no pleasure cruise, going to Kjerkfjorden," Arnar grumbled.

"I'm sturdier than I look," Julia told him, grinning.

"Why do you want to go to that shrine?" Arnar asked. "There are other ones. Better ones. Ones that aren't so shadowed."

Lars shook his head. "Don't let him scare you off. Arnar has already agreed. He's just being a curmudgeon about it."

"I'm charging double."

"We're taking *my* ship," Lars countered.

"You want me to take the wheel of that thing," Arnar said, looking as if he wanted to spit, "I should charge you triple."

"Arnar and Gale used to explore together," Lars said.

Julia turned in her chair. "You know Gale?"

Arnar cracked a smile, "*Ja.* Caves, old ruins, hidden lakes. Gale and me, we explored them all. Nora too. She was fearless. There wasn't a spot in this land that our youthful feet didn't touch. His whole life, Gale was convinced that the fjords and mountains held secrets."

"And do they?" Julia asked.

Arwar smiled, which was when Julia noticed he was missing one of his bottom teeth. "They do, madam. And they prefer to keep those secrets, secret."

35

Julia was back at her cabin before dawn had started streaking the sky. She went inside to fix herself another cup of coffee, bringing it out again and sitting contently on the front steps.

Julia loved sunrises; she always had.

It was, she found, even easier to love sunrises when they came at nine in the morning. Swathed in layers, she sat on her cabin's front step, a cup of hot coffee warming her hands, enjoying the play of colors across the sky, the way the sun crept ever upwards, chasing away shadows. Sky lay behind her, his body nestled warmly against her back. She had to call Harry to let the others know to pack some extra gear, but for now ... for now there was the sunrise.

There are worse ways to spend a morning.

When her coffee cup was empty and the sun was a little higher in the sky, Julia went into the little cabin and called Harry, ready to apologize for waking her at such an hour.

"Julia?" Harry said—she didn't sound remotely sleepy.

"Harry, what are you doing up? It's"—she looked at her watch—"it's got to be four in the morning there. I was ready to leave a voicemail."

"It's Lily," Harry said. "She's gone missing."

Julia's stomach plummeted and she sat down hard on the little couch. Sky hopped up beside her and Julia let her hand get lost in the soft, dense fur. "What? Missing? How?"

"That's what we're trying to find out. We don't know if there was an accident, if she defected, or, God forbid, if she was kidnapped."

Julia swallowed hard. "Let me know when you hear something. If she was—if she was taken, someone may try to get in touch with you. There might be a ransom, or—or something." It was all too surreal. *Ransom* was the kind of word you heard thrown around in movies and TV shows. It wasn't real life.

Except now it was.

"We just got Reg, Dai-Lu, and Betty on a plane. Francois and Reg are staying with me for now. He's making sure the computer system is completely locked down. We're taking every precaution, just in case."

"Good," Julia said, swallowing hard. "Please let me know if anything changes. Let me know if Lily turns up."

"You'll be the first to know."

Not long after Julia's call with Harry ended, there came a soft knock at the cabin door. She peeked through one of the front windows and spied James out front. Julia opened the door and ushered him in.

"Lily's missing," she said, without preamble.

"Lily is?" James asked, surprised. "What happened?"

Julia shook her head. "Harry isn't sure. She's not even sure whether Lily going missing was accidental or ... not."

Sky lifted his head to look at James and hopped off the sofa to greet him. But as James reached down to pet Sky, the dog sidled away, ducking his head.

"What's wrong, Sky?" James asked, reaching out to pet him again. Again, Sky ducked away. He turned around and went back to his spot on the sofa, tail tucked around him.

"That's unusual," Julia observed. "What's up, Sky? Snubbing James because he didn't bring you food?"

Sky didn't move; he just lay on the couch.

"Don't take it too personally," Julia said. "He may have just had his fill of socializing this morning."

"Socializing?" James asked.

Julia nodded and filled him in on her visit with Lars and Arnar.

"You ought to have woken me," he said. "I'm sorry to have missed that."

"I tried telling you last night, but you must've been in the bath. I knocked, but you didn't answer." She sent him a teasing smirk. "Unless you were entertaining a hot date?"

"Hardly," James replied. His tone was sharper than usual, and Julia backed off.

"I'm only kidding. Are you feeling well? You seem on edge."

James waved her question away and shook his head. "I'm fine. Just looking forward to putting this place behind us."

"Well, take the next couple of days to rest up and prepare. We'll be getting company soon and, with some skill and a bit of luck, you may just get your wish."

36

Reine Village, Lofoten archipelago

No sooner had Betty, Dai-Lu, and Reg arrived than they gathered their gear and marched down to the docks to load themselves and their gear on to Lars's ship, the Nordstjernen. It was a large, sturdy vessel, very obviously designed for fishing charters. Lars and Arnar, for all that they seemed to bicker the last time Julia saw them, appeared to have reached a détente, if nothing else. They argued good naturedly about the best route and how long it would take.

"I say forty-five minutes," Lars told Julia. "Arnar says an hour."

Betty pulled her hood up against the wind and sea spray. "Thirty minutes," she said. Both men looked at her and she shrugged. "I'm from New England. I grew up on boats."

Arnar poked Lars with his elbow. "Her, I like."

After watching Betty show off her seafaring skills for the next 30 minutes, Julia checked in with the others. She found James first, and he looked positively green.

She pulled off her glove and put a hand to his forehead. It was clammy. "Are you okay?"

"Not currently," James replied, trying to put on a stiff upper lip and, in Julia's opinion, failing. "I'll be right as rain once we're on land again."

"According to Arnar, that's going to be pretty soon. In fact, here he comes now," said Julia.

Arnar approached the group. "This is as far as we safely go. Lars will take you the rest of the way. I will be back for you in three days."

"What if we need you sooner?"

"Not to worry—I have flares if we need to signal Arnar sooner," Lars said, clapping his friend on the shoulder. "You're sure you don't want to come with us?"

"Tell me if you find him. That is all I want to know. I do not need to see what you find."

The whole group—Julia and Sky, James, Betty, Dai-Lu, and Reg, followed Lars off the boat, wading through the shore's shallow, cold waters.

"Be grateful," Lars called back to them. "The water could be even colder than it is!"

He led them onto dry land, where they all changed into hiking boots and, more importantly, dry socks.

"Are you ready?" Lars asked them.

"We are," Julia answered. She paused, looking around before adding, "All of us."

Less than fifteen minutes into their hike, Julia was increasingly grateful for the fitness room at the IFDC. She was doubly glad she'd made good use of the climbing wall. Her body did as she asked it to, which was a rare enough thing these days. It wasn't an easy hike, not by a long shot—and from the way her colleagues were breathing harder and harder, and occasionally swearing very creatively, Julia had a feeling they agreed with her.

Despite the fact that they had no idea what, if anything, they were going to find—it was an unmistakably beautiful locale. Their first break, roughly an hour in, Julia stood on a rocky outcropping and stared out at the craggy mountain ranges. The water was so still, so glassy, the mountains' reflections were nearly perfect.

I'll come back here, she promised herself. I'll come back here for a proper vacation, away from everyone and everything.

As they hiked, Sky gradually inched to the front of the line, walking alongside Lars. It gave Julia the chance to watch Sky interact with someone else. He was always by her side lately—she was used to the canine presence, but it wasn't until now, watching Sky walk with someone else, that she realized how . . . intuitive this dog was.

She thought back to the sailor who'd lost fingers to this same dog. This dog that walked by Lars' side, sniffing the ground and almost—almost making turns before Lars took them.

What are you sniffing out, Sky?

They took yet another rest on a granite platform above the Kjerkfjorden caves.

"It's just about noon," Lars told them. "We have roughly four hours of daylight left. I propose we continue on for another hour or two before stopping to break camp for the night."

"Are you sure that's wise?" James asked.

"The terrain will only become more challenging," Lars replied. "If you knew this mountain, were familiar with it—then yes, we could continue the journey in lower light. I will not take that chance with this group."

Lars was as good as his word. By 4:00 PM, the last vestiges of sunlight were fading from orange to pink to dusky purple. By the time they finished pitching tents and building a fire, it was nighttime.

They ate and cleaned up after themselves and discussed strategy for the next day.

"We will reach the entrance to Frigg's shrine tomorrow. I do not know what you expect to find there, but I suggest you prepare yourself for anything."

Once everyone had turned in for the night, Julia pulled the satellite phone out of her backpack and, very quietly, dialed Harry's number.

"You have no idea how glad I am you have the common sense to check in," Harry said by way of greeting.

"We're nearly to Frigg's shrine," Julia said. "We lost the light so we had to make camp."

"Not surprising—shorter days in that part of the world this time of year. How's the group doing?"

Julia gnawed her lip. Harry interpreted her silence as well as if Julia had spoken the words outright.

"Your hesitation tells me something isn't right."

"It's James," she said, keeping her voice to nearly a whisper. "Something's off. I can't tell what. It could be nothing."

"What do you call 'nothing'?"

"Sky's avoiding him," Julia told her, feeling foolish as she said it.

"Interesting," Harry replied. "I mean, if it were my sister in-law's Dachshund I'd say it had a personality problem. But Sky's a different kind of dog."

"But he's just a dog."

"Dogs can be better judges of people than people are," Harry said. "Keep an eye out. Could be nothing, might be something. And I'd rather you be aware if it turns out to be something. Anyone else acting squirely?"

"No," Julia said, shaking her head. "And for whatever it's worth, Sky hasn't been avoiding any of them."

"Good to know."

"Has there been any news about Lily?"

"Not yet. We're doing our best, but she's nowhere to be found." Harry paused and sighed. "I don't want to think the worst, but . . . "

"Maybe something will turn up," Julia said. "Stranger things have happened."

"I'll do my best," Harry replied. "Now go on, get some sleep. You'll want to be rested for tomorrow."

Julia hung up and put the satellite phone back in her backpack before snuggling down into her sleeping bag. Sky lay pressed against her leg. As she drifted off to sleep, one thought kept circling her mind:

Is the worst-case scenario if Lily betrayed us, or if she was taken against her will?

Her sleep was deep and dreamless and offered no answers.

37

Kjerkfjorde Caves, Norway

Julia woke to the sound of someone tending the campfire. She poked her head out and saw Lars feeding the flames. He looked incredibly well-rested—well enough that Julia wondered how often he came to this area to camp.

He looked up as Sky pushed his way out of the tent. "Good morning, Julia. Sleep well?"

She climbed out of the tent and stretched. "Do you want the truth?"

Lars chuckled. "I can probably guess the truth."

"In that case, I slept like a baby," she said, grinning.

It didn't take long for the other team members to wake up and start breaking camp. They kept the fire going, both for warmth and for light, since sunrise was still two hours off. It might have been helpful to use more of the portable lighting they'd packed, but it was vital they used their supplied mindfully. So, they did the best they could with the campfire and the small personal LED lanterns Betty, Reg, and Dai-Lu had brought.

"We'll start once we have light," Lars told them as they all sat around the campfire, drinking coffee and breaking their fast on trail mix and energy bars. "It will get more complicated from here on out. The path down to Frigg's shrine is in a cave opening further up the mountain. From there, the trail will lead downward again."

Sky rested his head on Julia's lap. She gave him an almond, which he crunched on happily.

Once camp was broken and everyone loaded up with their gear, the second leg of the trip began. But they'd only gone half a mile when Sky started veering to the left where Lars wanted to go right.

"Come on, boy, this way," Julia said. But Sky only stood still, watching her a moment before turning his head resolutely to the left.

"What is over that way?" Betty asked Lars.

"I truly don't know." Lars replied. "People come camping up here in the warmer months. It could be he's scenting another campsite."

"How much time will we lose if we head that way?" Julia asked.

Lars shook his head. "That depends on how far that way he leads us."

"You get ten minutes that way," Julia told Sky, firmly. "Ten minutes. That's it. Then we go *this* way."

Sky cocked his head.

Julia nodded. "Go."

"Are we sure Sky isn't a descendent of Lassie?" Reg muttered as they followed Sky off the trail.

It didn't take ten minutes, which didn't really surprise Julia at all.

Sky led them to another cave opening. He paused momentarily before continuing inside, his nose to the ground. Julia wondered if he'd found another campsite, but it wasn't anything like a campsite.

"This looks like someone's home," Dai-Lu said, looking around. She snapped on her LED light. "Or it was. It's hard to tell if anyone's been here recently."

The cave wasn't very deep. At one end was something that looked like it could have been a bed, fashioned out of grass. Beyond that, it was impossible to tell very much about the room; it was a mess. Papers and books littered every available surface. An overturned inkwell had spilled its dark contents onto a tattered map, and a teetering pile of scrolls threatened to tumble from its rickety shelf. The desk, if one could call it that, in the room's center was nearly buried under layers of parchment and very-possibly handmade quills. Runic markings covered the walls—some painted, some scrawled in charcoal. Atop the desk's mess was an aged piece of parchment with a drawing of a woman on it.

"That's Nora," Lars said quietly. "This is—this must be where Gale—"

James began sifting through the papers and opening scrolls. "It's a record," he said. "Of Gale's time here." He read a little longer, shaking his head. "If his dates are correct, he left this site yesterday, but was planning to return."

Lars hung his head and let out a long sigh. "I had hoped we would have found him alive," he said. "I will tell Arnar. Gale was his friend."

A voice broke the silence, a guttural growl of a voice—the voice of a man who hadn't spoken to another living being in years. "Don't speak about me like I'm dead. I've got life in me yet, damn it."

At the mouth of the cave was an old man, his body thin, but corded with wiry muscles. His hair was grey and long, pulled away from his face into a braid. He held in his hand a spear, and showed absolutely no hesitation about potentially using it.

"*Gale*," Lars exclaimed. "How—*how*?"

"Lars Nilsen. *Lars Nilsen.* Why take his appearance, you evil bastard? Why—" Gale stepped further into the cave, spear held aloft. Every word he spoke grew louder; his voice trembled and his eyes widened as he shouted until spittle flew from his lips. "Why? You took my Nora. Wasn't that enough? *Why?*"

Lars put his hands up, placating the older man. "Gale. It is me. It is Lars."

"*Liar!* You are *draugr!*"

Lars shook his head, standing perfectly still. "I am not. I am alive. I am flesh and blood."

Gale didn't move. "You lie. You always *lie to me!*"

"If I were truly *draugr,*" Lars said, his voice low and soothing, "would I stand so still? Would I keep my hands up? I bleed, Gale. I will show you that I bleed."

The arm supporting the spear trembled. "You . . . are Lars?" Gale whispered. The furious spittle clung to his lips; his eyes were still so wide Julia saw the whites around blue irises. "Not . . . not *draugr*?"

Slowly, the spear came down and Julia breathed again.

"We are not *draugr,*" Julia said. "None of us are."

Gale nodded absently. "Not *draugr.* Good. Good." He blinked, and in that time Gale's demeanor shifted again. No longer furious, he now smiled at Lars. "It's true, I am alive. Do you really think I would let this place kill me?" He shook his head. "It has taken too much from me already. My wife." He paused. "My mind. I won't let it take my life, too." Gale looked at the group huddled in his home, then back at Lars. "Who are these strangers in my home?"

Julia stepped forward. "Lars is taking us to Frigg's shrine."

Gale shook his head. "Don't. Don't, unless you have nothing else to lose." Gale's fingers clenched and released and for a moment Julia wondered if he'd take up the spear again. "I had too much to lose. I lost it. I lost it all."

Julia looked back at the others before facing Gale again. "We have plenty to lose. But we also think we know something about the shrine."

Interest suddenly sparked in Gale's pale eyes. "You know how to get in?"

"Possibly."

"My wife—my Nora's in there. I will bring you there if you get me inside."

38

Gale's habitat was surprisingly well-stocked, all things considered. He had a stockpile of handmade torches and some rudimentary weapons for defense and to catch food. It didn't take long for him to prepare. He'd been doing little else in his time living there.

"Gale," Lars began, watching the old man shove supplies in a battered rucksack. "Why did you believe me to be *draugr*?"

Gale flinched and swatted something away near his head. "I did not," he said. "I did not," he said again, through clenched teeth.

Dai-Lu appeared by Julia's side to whisper in her ear. "Are we sure this is a good idea?" Julia shook her head. There was very little she was sure of in this instant, beyond their need to reach Frigg's shrine.

"Gale," Lars tried again. "Why did you believe me to be such a monster?"

Gale dropped the rucksack. "They have been coming to me. The *draugr*."

A thick, skeptical silence followed, and Gale gritted his teeth. *He's lucid enough to know when people doubted him, at least,* thought Julia.

"After Nora was—after she was gone, I searched the caves, the mountains, the valleys, looking for her. I stayed there. The longer I stayed, the more I knew I needed to . . . stay." He gestured around his living area. "I found these things. I took them." His eyes darted left to right, nervously. "They were not mine to take."

"What do you mean," James asked, "you *found* them?"

"There are burial mounds around these lands," Lars said quietly. He turned to Gale. "That's what happened, isn't it?"

"But it's clearly not an *actual* monster after him," James argued.

In a blur of movement, Gale's hands fisted in James's coat, and he roared in James's face; color mottled the old man's cheeks like fever. "*Do not tell me when* ***you*** *do not know.*"

"*Draugr,*" Lars explained patiently, "do not like their graves disturbed. Gale may have taken an heirloom or the deceased's favorite knife."

"I do not know what I took that angered them," Gale said, releasing his grip and turning back to his half-packed bag. "All I know is I killed one of their number, and they taunt me to this day."

James looked around at the group. "And we're *okay* with this?"

Reg wrestled for a moment, clearly trying to find a fitting reply. "I think, if Gale has been living in this locale *by himself*, then we ought not to overlook a potentially helpful resource."

"That is why we have a *guide*," James spat.

Julia stepped in front of James. When he spoke, she kept her voice low. "This is what we're doing, James," she said, her tone brooking no argument. "If you have a problem with it, go down to the shore and wait for us. Otherwise, pull yourself together."

A series of emotions rippled across James's face; one of them, Julia was certain, looked a lot like hatred. She didn't move, didn't look away, didn't give any ground.

Finally, after too many seconds ticked past, James exhaled and turned away. "Fine. I'll stay."

Gale and Lars led the way. In one hand, Gale held a torch, its flames casting long, undulating shadows on the damp cave walls. As he moved, the rugged surfaces flickered with a golden hue.

Beside Julia, Sky's nostrils flared with rapid short inhalations and long, forceful exhales. Julia breathed in, trying to smell what Sky did, trying to taste the air—but all she identified was a strong metallic, mineral scent at first. Gradually she became aware of another odor, beneath the minerals: rot and decay from forgotten tide pools.

A few yards further, Gale paused. "We are here," he said.

Before them lay an expansive chamber, the ceiling lost to the shadows above, and at its center was a very large, very still tide pool.

"The goddess Frigga," Gale said, "was said to live beneath these waters. The stories said she watched over mothers and children and protected them from dangerous tribes of wandering trolls."

"According to legend," Lars added, "there is a doorway at the bottom of the pool through which she spirits away those she protects."

"What lies beyond?" Reg asked.

"The only ones who know that are the ones she takes inside," Gale replied, not a little bitterly.

Julia crouched, touching her fingers to the water's surface; as it rippled, she saw something at the bottom of the pool. "What's that?" she asked. "It looks like—it looks like a rune."

Betty joined her, an LED light ready. "What kind of rune? What's it look like?" she asked.

"An X, I think."

Betty thrust her light into the pool; it pushed away just enough of the gloom to show an X at the bottom of the pool. "That's Gebo!" she cried. "A gift—or sacrifice. It can also indicate a sacred union—as in marriage or family." Betty looked at Julia, excitement lighting her eyes. "That's one of the words from the Eemian map," she whispered. "I didn't know if it meant an offering or a sacrifice."

"What if it's both?" Julia asked.

"I'm starting to think it's both," Betty agreed.

Before anyone could say anything more, Gale waded into the pool and ducked beneath the water to press the rune.

"Gale!" Lars yelled when the older man surfaced again. "Are you *mad*?"

"Yes," he answered simply. "And I'm getting inside that thriece damned shrine." He climbed out of the pool, dripping wet. Slowly the water drained out of the pool, revealing a hatch at the bottom. Gale shimmied back down to the bottom of the pool. He pulled at the hatch door to no effect.

Muttering what Julia could only guess were Norwegian swear words, Lars joined Gale at the bottom of the pool and helped him pull at the hatch.

With a deafening groan, the door opened, revealing a stairway leading downward into darkness.

39

Green River Formation, Colorado

A cool dampness settled across the mesa. To the north, the rims of the ancient weather-worn hills were fringed with a pink hue as the sun slipped quietly away to end another day.

Magnus stepped down from the truck cab and surveyed his surroundings. Patches of brown sagebrush and the occasional outcrop of blotchy red lichen-covered rock punctuated the mesa. To the east, the snowcapped Rockies glistened in the late afternoon sun. Below him, the blast site was a flurry of activity. A line of ten double-bottom "belly dump" trucks waited to follow the foreman's instructions and drive over the gaping pit, dropping their fifty-ton loads of ammonia nitrate. Magnus watched in fascination as a bright orange double trailer positioned itself over the pit and released its contents in a billowing cloud of white before moving a few feet forward and repeating the process with its second trailer.

"Where are they in the delivery schedule?" asked Magnus.

"Last I checked," said Grimes, "we've received close to fifteen hundred belly dumpers. We'll have all two thousand loaded into the site by tomorrow."

No sooner had the orange trailer rumbled out of the dump zone than a second took its place. More clouds of white erupted from the pit. In the distance, a line of trucks bounced up the dirt road to join the dumpers ready to release their loads.

Grimes pulled his eyes from the line of trucks and focused them on Magnus. "This sure is going to make one hell of a bang when we light that fuse."

"The power of an atomic bomb using nothing more than crop fertilizer," said Magnus. "Who'd have thought?"

"We're going to shake things up around here," said Grimes.

"That's what we're all hoping for," said Magnus.

Magnus's attention shifted from the dumpers to a white pickup truck with green and yellow markings on its side parked by the command building. The Garfield County Sheriff vehicle pulled away from the trailer and headed up the dirt road out of the site, leaving a spume of red dust in its wake.

"Have you seen all the protesters at the main entrance fence?" asked Grimes.

"They won't get anywhere near this site."

"Says Tommy? Boss, I'm not sure ... well. I'm not sure I'd let him get so close to things, if I were you."

Magnus felt the weight of Grimes's stare on the side of his face. Some things weren't for John to know. Not anymore. "You're not me," said Magnus.

40

The noonday sun felt good against Magnus's back as he stood atop a small hill overlooking the valley floor. Below him, a growing swarm of protesters crowded the fences keeping them at bay.

"Looks to be quite a crowd," said Jack, peering through a pair of binoculars.

She placed the binoculars in his hand when he reached for them. He didn't think he was imagining the way her fingertips lingered just a moment longer than necessary, but when he glanced at her face, her expression was smooth and serene. With her hair pulled back in a ponytail, he had a great view of her slender neck. To keep himself from wondering what it would be like to kiss that neck, he lifted the binoculars and scanned the throngs below. At the front of the crowd, protesters carried black placards that read MASS EXTINCTION, STOP THE FRACKING, and SAVE THE PLANET. Closest to the fence he could see three women dressed in black with their faces painted white, their eyes and noses black with lips like a Calaveras mask. Behind them stood a person dressed in a red Santa Claus outfit wearing a black gas mask. To his side, two white-robed grim reapers chanted and milled about, holding signs in the air that read FRACKING KILLS!

"They look angry," said Magnus.

His scan of the crowd stopped at a small group of demonstrators dressed like ghosts—or maybe Ku Klux Clansmen—carrying placards that sent shivers down his spine. BURN IN HELL SAWYER! and KILL SAWYER BEFORE HE KILLS US!

Jack smiled and bumped her shoulder against his. "They're safely behind that fence, Magnus. You've got nothing to worry about. We've spared no expense on security, and all publicity is good publicity. Just think—these same people will be singing your praises when they realize everything you've done for them."

Together, they climbed up the grated-metal steps into the command trailer. Inside, two tripod-mounted television cameras and a pack of reporters were crowded into the cramped space.

Even if the crowd might not have parted for him, they stepped aside for Jack. She bestowed magnanimous smiles upon them all, like a goddess appreciating the gifts of her supplicants. He was grateful when she didn't leave him alone in front of the crowd, though she did step back, hovering behind his shoulder like the proverbial angel.

Suppose that makes Tommy the devil.

"Thank you all for coming this afternoon," said Magnus, patting away the beads of sweat forming on his brow with the back of his sleeve. "I think there's some cold coffee and a few week-old doughnuts in the little break area behind you. Feel free to help yourself. Here at Empire, we spare no expense."

The room erupted in laughter as Jack closed the door of the trailer and joined those standing in the press area.

"Welcome to you all." Magnus scanned the tightly packed room. "I'd like to start with a bit of background, and then we can cover the details of the project. We'll end by answering any questions you might have."

Cameras flashed and the television rig lit Magnus's face.

"On September 9th, 1969, the United States Department of the Interior, along with the Atomic Energy Commission and the Texas-based Astral Oil Company, detonated a forty-kiloton nuclear device not more than one hundred miles from here. Not many folks know that. I know I was surprised when I learned about it."

None of the reporters looked particularly surprised.

He cleared his throat. "That test, designed to see if they could extract natural gas, brought hundreds of protesters from all over the nation: concerned citizens worried about radiation contaminating their drinking water. Now, those folks? They were right to be worried. Subsequent testing showed unacceptable levels of radioactive contamination in the water table."

"Looks like things haven't changed that much," quipped one of the reporters. "Will you be addressing the concerns of the protesters outside today?"

Magnus inclined his head. "I think a lot of folks out there today are worried that we're gonna make things worse—but that couldn't be farther from the truth. See, we're not making the mistakes they made back in 1969. No, sir, we are not. We've learned. We know how important it is to break away from fossil fuels and cut back on carbon emissions. My own son's been from one end of the Earth to the other studying the effects we've had on the environment, and—"

"He's Dr. Samuel Sawyer, correct? University of Texas?" a voice called out.

Magnus's lips trembled with the effort required to hold on to his smile. "He's still a doctor, all right, but now he's back where he belongs—at Empire. He's doing great things for us."

"So, he thinks this is the right thing for the environment? He supports your decision to engage in fracking? At the cost of the parkland above it? Even though—"

Jack stepped forward. "Sir, if you'd be so kind as to hold your questions until the end of the presentation, we'd appreciate it."

Magnus gave her a grateful nod. "Thank you, Ms. Henley. Now ... where was I?"

"The process," Jack said softly, returning to her spot behind him.

"Right you are. Now, here's the difference between those first attempts and our method. Traditional means of gas and oil extraction rely upon hydraulic fracturing, a process that is neither safe nor environmentally friendly. It uses enormous amounts of water, and emits greenhouse gases, brine, and toxic fracturing fluids. Traditional fracking contaminates water, causes noise pollution, and often results in health issues. Why, some folks too close to a hydraulic fracking site have had their water faucets light on fire."

Magnus put his hands up to quiet the grumbles of the press.

"That ain't happenin' here," he said, laying his Texan accent on thick. "Our thermal extraction method is safe and environmentally friendly. Hell, come back here in a couple of days and I'll drink straight from the nearest stream without so much as a pause of concern."

"Sounds like a load of hogwash to me," muttered someone else. "Environmentally friendly *gas?* Pull the other one."

"I hear you," Magnus said. "I was just as skeptical when Dr. Ethan Pickens darkened my door nearly six months ago. Near turned him down flat. But then he explained the process. And, hell, that process is airtight. Give me a moment to explain, and I think you'll come around to my way of thinking."

He didn't *really* think the naysayer would come around, but the rest of the crowd tittered and turned their rapt gazes right where he wanted them—on him. On the words Pickens had drilled into him until he could repeat them forward and backward. "This is how it goes. We drill a shaft nearly two miles deep into the ground. We load tens of thousands of tons of *conventional* explosive materials, like those used in commercial mining—no atom-splitting here, folks—and in a single explosion, we generate temperatures high enough to vaporize the surrounding rocks. This extreme and sudden heat creates a massive spherical underground cavern.

"Some of the ceiling of this newly formed cave is unstable and, as soon as things start to cool down, the inside of the giant room collapses onto itself, forming a chimney of fractured rocks—rocks that once trapped millions of cubic feet of natural gas that can now be released. We then drill a second shaft into the chimney, and out comes clean, natural gas for years to come."

The lack of grumbling only drove Magnus onward. "Now here's

the magic of it. During this entire process we haven't used one *drop* of water—except the kind we give our guys out there to keep 'em comfortable under the sun. There's no contamination, and the only environmental impact of any kind is a single explosion that shakes the ground for no more than ten seconds."

Out of the corner of his eye, Magnus saw Jack giving him the gesture to bring the speech to a close.

"Once we verify the shot has gone as planned, we bring in a feeder pipeline from the main trunk and begin delivering clean, environmentally friendly natural gas to help America with its energy needs."

"What about these explosions causing sink holes and damaging tectonic plates?" asked a reporter near the back of the small room.

"That's a great question, sir, and I appreciate you askin' it," said Magnus. "Fact is, the intensity of the heat from the explosion fuses solid the walls of the newly formed cavern. About three quarters of that new wall collapses under its own weight—that's where we get all that natural gas. The remaining quarter is about as thick as you might find in the strongest of any building man has ever made. Those walls'll be standin' strong from now to the end of time."

Cameras clicked and flashes lit Magnus's face.

"As for tectonic plates"—Magnus grinned from ear to ear—"those hunks of land that we stand on are about 75,000 miles thick. Our little scratch wouldn't even register."

"What about the climate crisis?" asked one of the local reporters. "You can't say these new wells won't add to the carbon load."

"Now, now, ma'am," said Magnus. "You're right. There's carbon in natural gas, but its a whole lot less than in oil or coal. And that's the problem, ain't it? Folks today just want some sort of magic wand to make everything okay. Well, that'd be great, but last time I checked we were runnin' short on wands." The room erupted into laughter. "Now, I don't mean to make light of your question. It's a good one. We all need to be workin' hard to cut our carbon emissions. And Empire's doing exactly that with our natural gas wells. Natural gas has half the carbon of oil and coal. It's clean energy, ma'am, clean energy."

"What about the protesters?" asked one of the reporters near the front of the crowd. "They want to know why Empire Energy isn't focusing on renewables."

"We like renewables," said Magnus. "Sure we do. And when renewables alone can power America, I promise I'll be the first in line to use them. Until then, Empire's working to keep America's machinery running and our lights on. We're workin' to power the offices of the folks who'll one day bring us viable alternatives to our natural gas. More importantly, ma'am, if America supplies its own energy, we can say goodbye to—pardon my crudeness and my pun—bein' held over the barrel by folks that don't live in this country, don't uphold our values. And that's a real positive. We call our own shots from here on out."

Jack stepped gracefully to the podium and gifted the crowd with another of her beatific smiles. "That's all we have time for this afternoon, but I hope you're not planning on leaving. We have quite a show planned for you tonight."

41

Kjerkfjorde Caves, Norway

JULIA EXCHANGED LOOKS WITH DAI-LU, Betty, Reg, and James.

"This is it," she said. "The point of no return. If any of you have misgivings of any kind or want to turn back for any reason, now is the time to do it. There'll be no judgment from me."

"With respect, Julia," Reg said, "I think all of us came here with eyes open. Or we damn well tried to. I'm not turning back now. We've come too far."

Betty nodded. "Besides, there's a good chance you'll need me down there."

"I'm not giving up now," Dai-Lu said, firmly.

"James?" Julia prompted.

He'd looked better. "I won't turn back now. There's too much at stake."

With Gale in the lead, still holding his torch, which he'd managed to keep burning, they walked down the stairs, single file. Reg closed the hatch behind them, and if not for their torches and lanterns, they'd have been plunged into complete darkness.

The stairs led down, down, down, turning this way then that, so far down, Julia wondered just how far below the water's surface they were.

"Gale?" Julia asked.

"What is it?" he called back.

She looked around them. The walls of this tunnel were too smooth, too perfectly formed to be natural. And yet too old to have been crafted with modern tools. The passage seemed to go on forever, but there was no echo—their footfalls barely made any sound at all. "How ... just how did your wife go missing?"

He sighed. "Is this the time for such a story?"

"At what point did she vanish?"

"I will let you know when we reach that point. I will never forget it as long as I live."

"Julia," Dai-Lu said from behind her, her voice low. "Have you noticed the walls?"

"Is it graphene?" Julia asked.

"No—not the material," she said. "I mean, have you noticed the *mural.*"

Jerking her lantern up, Julia looked at the wall to her right—sure enough, there was a representation of a goddess, most likely Frigg, leading pregnant women and children into a tidepool while Ragnarök raged behind them.

The mural continued as they descended, depicting all the horrors of Ragnarök—volcanoes, fires, floods. All the Aesir were depicted, deep in battle amid fireballs and floodwaters. Further along in the mural, all the gods and goddesses of the Norse pantheon were shown, bloody and defeated, the Earth burned as the rains flooded what remained.

"It looks like Frigg, in this representation, protects the future generations so there's life to repopulate the new world after Ragnarök," Betty said.

"So what's the catch?" Dai-Lu asked. "What's the 'gift'?"

"Or the sacrifice?" Julia asked.

Finally, after what felt like an eternity of walking, they reached the bottom of the stairway. A short tunnel opened up to a wide cavernous opening. At the far end were two enormous, intricately carved doors. As they drew closer, it became evident the doors showed the story that had been depicted in the mural: Frigg leading mothers and children away from the devastation of Ragnarök.

Julia moved closer and peered at Frigg. There was something eerily familiar about the goddess's appearance. She brushed her fingers over the carving and gasped.

In one of Sam's photos of the Eemian sanctuary, there was a portrait of a family. Frigg bore a racial resemblance to the people in that portrait. A strong resemblance.

"What is it?" Reg asked.

"Did you see all the images Sam took with his phone?"

Reg nodded, then moved closer to the door, scrutinizing the carvings. After a moment he jerked back, cursing quietly.

"You see it too," Julia said.

Reg nodded. "I do."

"I think our Frigg," Julia said softly, "is Eemian."

Gale raised a hand, signaling everyone to halt. Then he moved in close to the group, watching their faces, his unease evident. "Quiet now," he instructed in a hushed voice. "We're near the shrine. Can you feel it?"

Julia strained her ears, but the only sound she could hear was the collective breaths of their group and Sky's rhythmic panting.

With a nod, Lars indicated everyone's torches and lanterns. "Douse them, all of them," he said. Once the last torch was extinguished, the darkness pressed in on them. There was no light, anywhere. For a horrible, disorienting moment, Julia wasn't even sure which way was up. She'd heard about that befalling spelunkers—darkness so thick they couldn't right themselves. And despite the fact that she knew her own two feet were on the ground, she still wasn't sure which way was up.

Just when Julia was certain she couldn't take another second of that darkness, Gale's rough, hoarse voice broke the silence.

"*Frigg,*" he whispered. "We offer ourselves to you, goddess."

Something *changed* in that cavern.

42

Green River Formation, Colorado

It was early evening and Magnus's frame cast no shadow upon the desolate landscape. He looked beyond the endless field of tumbleweeds and scrub bushes covering the richest deposit of natural gas on the planet to the hills north of where he stood. There, a deep blanket of purple just above the distant hilltops met the darkening gray of twilight. To the southwest, Venus twinkled. Mars would soon be visible too. At this altitude—over a mile high—and without the pollution of city lights, the splash of visible planets and stars would normally light the heavens. Not tonight. If all went as planned, the Milky Way would give way to the blazing light of the riches once buried deep within the Earth.

And then the money would start rolling in. He'd buy off Tommy. Hopefully, Jack would stick around.

For once, the ghost of Henry Sawyer had nothing to say. No criticism to give. No snide remark to make.

Tonight, they would celebrate the success of the world's first explosive-based thermal extraction natural gas wellhead by lighting the night sky so bright they'd see it as far away as Denver. Their victory lap. Tommy Jones had wanted a show, and Magnus had every intention of giving him one.

He planned on making it a goodbye party to remember.

From behind him came the crunch of tires, the sigh of an airbrake, and the opening and closing of a door. A moment later, Tommy stood at Magnus's side, smug as ever. "Told you the protesters wouldn't be a problem," Tommy said.

"Night's not over yet," said Magnus.

Tommy snorted. "Always the pessimist, Sawyer. You got the whole world handed to you on a silver—hell, a Texas gold platter, and you still look around and only see the shit that hasn't gone your way." Tommy glanced up at him slantwise. "Hope you come back as a five-foot-six son of a used car salesman, next time around. Maybe then you'll understand how the world works for guys like me."

"Now, now, Tommy. The Lord doesn't truck with this multiple lives nonsense. I think I'm safe."

"That's the problem with you, Sawyer. You walk through the world stepping on folks like me, and then you have the gall to still look down on us when we save your ass time and again." Tommy turned his face up to the sky. "Y'know, Magnus, I've a mind to change the terms of our deal. See, I've been lookin' for new digs. Thing is, the house I really want? It's occupied."

Magnus shuddered like someone was doing cartwheels over his grave. "You're not changing a damn thing."

"That's the other problem with you silver-spoon types. You think nothin' can change. You think you'll always be protected. But then you count on guys like me, who hate the bullies like you, to do that protectin'." Tommy laughed, almost to himself. "Being born rich makes people dumb, Sawyer. Makes 'em weak. Makes 'em forget who really calls the shots out there. Out here."

"You trying to threaten me, Jones?"

"No, sir," said Tommy. "Not *trying.* Just ... you know, doin' my job. Lookin' out for the bottom line." In the dark, the shorter man's smile was a flash of white. For a second, Magnus almost imagined pointed teeth, jaws that could rip out his throat. "Protectin' my investment, as it were."

Magnus hated himself for flinching when Tommy patted him on the arm.

"And if you ever *do* decide to sell that old place of your daddy's, I hope you'll give me the first right of refusal. For old time's sake, right? We monsters gotta look out for each other. Otherwise, hell, we're just liable to fall."

Before he could think up an adequately righteous response, Tommy stalked off into the dark, returning to his car. "Oh, and Magnus? I'll be making the speech tonight. I'll be the one lightin' the flame. And hell, if God is good, maybe I'll be the one between the delectable Jacqueline Henley's thighs." His laughter set Magnus's teeth on edge. "Maybe it was your name, but it was my millions."

43

Kjerkfjorde Caves, Norway

The space above them, once a solid dome of oppressive black, began a metamorphosis. Soft points of blue light, imperceptible at first, dotted the ceiling above. As Julia's eyes adjusted to the subtlety of the glow, she lost her breath at its beauty: a subterranean night sky. The organisms didn't merely shine; they pulsed, they moved, like stars shifting and realigning.

Like droplets of liquid starlight, the bioluminescent beings moved in harmony. The group below stood transfixed, their faces bathed in the gentle glow.

"It's amazing," Dai-Lu breathed. "Positively amazing."

The tall, intricately carved doors slowly opened. The blue glow faded back to darkness.

One by one, lanterns snapped back on. Beyond the doors was a vast chamber, the walls of which were decorated with more images of Frigg and her devotees—children playing happily in a new world, fresh, young, and green. Ragnarök had passed, and this was the era of rebirth.

At the end of that cavern was another set of doors, at least twelve feet high and ten feet wide. Its surface was a shade of deep black. Graphene, cold to the touch.

Taking off her gloves, Julia approached the door cautiously, her hand outstretched. She brushed her fingertips over the door and shivered—it was smooth but painfully cold to the touch. Hastily she pulled her gloves back on before touching the embedded characters.

Julia wondered if this was what Sam had seen in Antarctica. The characters were as precise as if they had been crafted by skilled hands or perhaps, as she had once theorized, by ancient machines. The door's surface felt like silk, impossibly smooth given its age and location.

"Do you think you can translate, Betty?" Julia asked, her voice steadier than she expected it to be.

Betty came forward and held up her light.

"It's the same character as before. The one that means either *gift, sacrifice,* or *offering.* But there's more here, too." She studied the door, hand covering her mouth. "I think it's actually *meant* to mean all three, simultaneously. The context here is so odd."

"Children," Julia said suddenly. "*Children.*"

Betty stepped back suddenly. "You might be right. Holy shit." She scanned the rest of the door. "Yes. That tracks. A child is a gift. But also—also parents sacrifice for their children. And here, if those murals are a hint, here children are offered to Frigg, so she can repopulate the world after Ragnarök."

"Are you trying to tell me that people sacrificed their children to Frigg?" James asked, skepticism heavy in his voice.

"No," Julia said, looking at Gale. "I don't think anyone sacrificed anything *knowingly.*"

Even in that dim light, Julia was sure the color had drained from Gale's face.

"Are you saying you think Nora was taken by Frigg?"

"I don't know what happened yet, but we're going to find out," said Julia. "Reg, help us out here."

Reg joined Julia and Betty at the door. It had two recessed horizontal levers, both designed for a two-handed grip. Their positioning and design hinted at some mechanism that, when activated, would allow passage. Reg grabbed one handle, while Betty and Julia grabbed the other. They pulled as hard as they could, to no avail.

Julia scanned the door's surface, searching for any sign of the unique patterns Sam had mentioned. Those conversations were so long ago now, she barely remembered the details. All she knew was that she didn't have that damned amulet.

He gave me his dog, he gave me the key to his apartment, but did he give me the thing I actually needed to get this door open? Signs point to no.

Lars and Gale's torches cast long, quivering shadows that flickered upon the door's surface, making their task even more challenging, as every symbol twisted and moved in the torchlight. The door's entire surface was an intricate tapestry of symbols, each deeply and perfectly etched into the cold, dark graphene. Some, she remembered, mirrored those on the amulet. Others were completely foreign to them. Sweat dripped from Lu's brow as she traced a series of symbols that seemed promising. But every lead turned cold. Every pattern they thought they recognized from the amulet seemed to distort upon closer inspection.

Running a hand through her hair, Julia sat on the ground. She had to think. There had to be a way to open this door. Brute force was out as an option, but something had to be available. She just had to think.

Sky padded over and sniffed at the top of her head.

"Thanks, buddy," she said, her head still buried in her hands. She looked up in time for Sky to lick her cheek. Julia smiled and reached up and patted the side of Sky's neck. The tags upon his collar jingled softly.

Wait. Tags?

There hadn't been time to do laundry, much less bring Sky to a vet for a city license and rabies tag. Julia peered closer at Sky's collar and gasped.

There, dangling from the thick leather, was Sam's Eemian amulet.

Sam Sawyer, she thought, *you and I are going to have a conversation when I get out of this.*

She unbuckled Sky's collar and pulled the amulet free. She pressed it hard into matching depression. Suddenly, the chamber reverberated with the sound of two heavy, metallic *thunks* originating from the door.

One more time, Julia and Reg grabbed the levers and pulled. The lever started to budge. James reached over and lent a third set of hands, and the lever clicked open. They looked at each other for the briefest of moments, then wrestled open the second, lower lever.

The ground trembled beneath them, and a gust of ancient, stale air rushed out as the door slowly slid open.

44

Green River Formation, Colorado

Tommy was ten feet tall and floating on cloud nine by the time he approached the staging grounds. Jack turned away from a conversation with one of the milling reporters and joined him.

"Did you find Magnus?" she asked. "We're all set to start."

Tommy shrugged. "Said he wasn't feeling well. He asked me to take over tonight."

She blinked at him, and the thrill of seeing her momentarily discomposed was almost a high. "Are you sure—"

"Come on now, Jackie. When have you seen me unsure about anything?" He threw her a wink. "I suppose Magnus has his boy Grimes manning the flame? You go tell him to get a small flame going and be ready for my signal. I want this place to light up like a Roman Candle."

He didn't wait for Jack to acknowledge him. She was a good girl; she'd get things done.

Tommy rolled his shoulders and cracked his neck before heading out to the podium that had been set up for him.

Showtime.

Twin LED floodlights pointed directly at Tommy.

"Ladies and gentlemen, members of the press, and especially everyone tuning in live, thank you for being with us on this monumental occasion. I'm Tommy Jones and I'm filling in for the CEO of Empire Energy, Magnus Sawyer. Mr. Sawyer's feeling a bit under the weather so you're all stuck with me."

A polite round of applause followed, but it only twisted his belly, made him burn for the respect and adoration he knew he deserved.

"How did America get so weak?" Tommy's voice rang out into dead silence. Somewhere, he knew Jack was shitting a brick. "How did our middle class, once the envy of the rest of the world, slip into the abyss of financial ruin? Is it because of the Wall Street gang? The oil barons, the ultra-rich billionaire-club members? Or is it because of those protesters who want us to stop energy production and save the planet without providing a single sane alternative?"

The chants of the protesters echoed up from below. Tommy turned his head in their direction and, for his audience, shook his head in disapproval.

"Truth is, we're all victims of the greatest power grab of all time. There are those outside our country so jealous of what we have that they want to take it away just for the satisfaction of seeing us suffer. Theirs is a calculated plan to break the back of this country, take what was once ours, and make us dependent on them to meet our needs."

The audience waited, hushed. He couldn't see their faces because of the light, but he didn't need to. They were rapt. They belonged to him.

"America spends nearly a trillion dollars each year purchasing energy from outside the borders of our great nation. You have any idea how much of that money goes to line the pockets of folks who outright hate our way of life? Folks who, if they had their way, wouldn't mind crushing us into the dust forever?"

The audience stirred. A few cheers rang out. Some intrepid soul started singing the national anthem at the top of his out-of-key lungs.

"Every war we've fought in my lifetime, my father's lifetime—wars that cost trillions of dollars and thousands of American lives—has been over energy. Today, we end that!"

Tommy leaned into the podium and spoke softly into the microphone that carried every nuance out across the darkened valley.

"This nation depends on energy to keep our industries running, our cars traveling, and our homes heated and cooled. By switching to clean *American* natural gas and leaving coal and oil buried in the ground, we're cutting emissions by more than half and still keeping the lights on."

This round of applause was louder. Better. More appreciative.

"My vision for America is here, right here," said Tommy, waving his hand toward the wellhead. "Without damaging the environment, we have opened a new source of clean energy for our country. When my people open that valve"—Tommy pointed to Grimes—"we'll light this party up so bright that they'll see us from a hundred miles away!"

The crowd was cheering now. Chanting his name. *His* name. Not Magnus Sawyer's. Not the President's. *His.*

"This is the answer to America's energy problems." Tommy spread his hands out toward the wellhead and flare stack. "Energy independence for a nation hungry for freedom and a world anxious to keep the lights on and food on the table."

Tommy placed the microphone in his left hand and with his right raised high over his head, waved at Grimes.

"For all the critics and naysayers out there," said Tommy, "let's turn the lights on high and show the world what American ingenuity can really do!"

The cameras all turned toward the flare stack. Grimes didn't move. Tommy clenched his jaw and pumped his fist into the air again. Grimes remained still, his arms folded over his chest.

Tommy threw the microphone to the ground and bounded over to the flare stack. The crowd roared. With all his strength, Tommy wrenched on the wheel. The flame got a little bigger, then bigger still, before holding steady at about five feet tall.

"Let's show the world what it means to mess with America!"

Grimes loomed over him, but Tommy wasn't going to be cowed by some Stetson-wearing old hick who should've retired years back.

Because maybe he was a monster, but he wasn't a fucking coward. With his back to the audience, knowing the flame would hide his actions, Tommy drew the weapon he'd been concealing. The gun was small, tiny even, but at this range? It was enough. The roar of the crowd—the reporters, the dignitaries, the protesters—covered the sound of the shot and John Grimes dropped to his knees, then slumped forward.

"That's right," Tommy hissed. "Sit down, old man. Take a load off. I'll handle this."

Tommy threw the full force of his weight, his rage, his desire at the crank. It held for a moment and then, instantaneously, night turned into day. A wash of heat flooded over him. For an instant, he shrank back from its intensity, but he didn't release the wheel. He turned it. Again. Again. More. It grew brighter and taller, reaching higher into the night sky. The crowd stopped their approach, and the cheers became screams as those nearest to the flame turned and ran from the searing heat.

More! More! Give me more! Give me everything you've got!

Tommy hands blistering from the heat of the metal, tilted his head back at a sky too bright for stars and laughed.

"This is for you, you foreign sons of bitches!" he shouted. "This is the power I have unleashed from the Earth. This is the power I control! This is who you're fucking with now!"

"Tommy!" shouted Magnus over the roar of the flame overhead. "Enough! It's big enough! Stop!"

"Fuck you, Sawyer! Fuck you and everyone like you! You don't deserve this! You never deserved any of it!" Tommy kept his head slung back, laughing, watching the flames soar into the heavens. Sweat ran in rivulets down his face. He was alive—more alive than he'd ever been. *More! More! This is mine! All mine! And I say let it burn!*

And then the darkness returned, but the stars were all gone.

45

Kjerkfjorde Caves, Norway, January, 22

The door hung open, darkness gaping beyond. Julia lifted her flashlight, but the gloom only swallowed up the beam.

"This." Gale said. "*This.*" His frame shook with such violent tremors that he sunk to the ground, hugging his knees. "This is where I lost her. You asked—*you asked me. This is where I lost Nora. Here here here*--" He rocked slowly, tilting his head back as he heaved great, wet sobs. Tears and snot ran down his face, gleaming in the lantern light.

James groaned outright. "Now? You thought *now* was the right time for a breakdown?"

"James," Julia snapped. It was enough. He subsided, however sulkily.

Lars knelt in front of Gale. Sky gave Julia's hand a brief lick before walking over to the older man and lying down behind him, pressing his furry body against Gale's back. "You led us here, Gale. You led us here and now we will find Nora."

"I led us here," he managed between sobs. "I did it. I led us here."

"And we're going to find Nora," Lars told him firmly.

Gale gave a shaky nod. "We're going to find her."

"If there are *draugr* here, we will face them and fight them together. *Ja?*"

Again, Gale nodded. After a few more moments, he pushed to his feet. "There is evil within," he said, though he was more subdued; the outburst had taken a lot out of him. "Frigg would not have taken my wife. She is a goddess. She protects, she doesn't take."

Julia looked at Betty, who nodded. "What is the difference between a gift, an offering, and a sacrifice when they're all described with the same rune?"

Stunned, Lars said, "An offering if you're the goddess, a sacrifice if you're the husband."

"Just so," Betty said.

As they stepped over the door's threshold, the atmosphere changed; the air got colder, and the antechamber behind them felt very far away indeed. They pushed onward, slowly, through the dark passageway, the cold grew more intense. Despite wearing multiple layers of warm clothing, a chill wormed its way through her clothes, all the way down to the marrow of her bones. Her teeth chattered as she hugged her arms against her body. She wondered if the others were as cold as she.

If not for the soft scuffles of their footsteps and Gale's sniffling whimpers, the silence combined with the cold might have been oppressive.

"The monsters will take us," Gale whispered despite Lars attempting to calm him. "I stole from their graves, and they will hunt me, hunt us all--"

Somewhere to Julia's right, James swore.

Reginald muttered, "Were you always utterly devoid of basic human empathy?"

James made an annoyed sound. "He's a *distraction,* and he's slowing us down. We need to keep up the bloody pace."

"I see." Reg walked a few seconds in contemplative silence. Then: "I'd hate to live in your world."

"Lucky for me you don't," James sniped.

"No," Reg replied. "Lucky for both of us."

Dai-Lu's voice came from Julia's other side. "I really hope this is worth it."

So do I, Julia answered silently.

As they made their way through the tunnel, the air changed yet again, growing strangely heavy, almost dense. But before Julia could think too much about it, the tunnel opened up into a cavernous space, the ceiling so high that their flashlight beams failed to pierce the darkness. Casting her beam around the room showed Julia enough. They had reached their destination.

"Okay," Julia said, "let's get the LEDs set up. We need some light in here to see what we're working with."

A flurry of activity followed. Different team members worked to set up a series of portable lights around them. The cavernous room was too vast to set up a perimeter of lights, which would have been ideal, but this measure eased away most of the gloom and revealed more to them than they could have imagined. Julia looked over her shoulder at Lars and Gale, who remained by the cavern's entrance, staring around them as the portable lighting uncovered mystery after mystery.

"Hey, Betty," Reg called across the space, "come over here. Look."

He was standing by one of the walls – it bore an intricate message comprised of varying characters and symbols. Reverently, Betty laid one gloved hand upon the engraving.

"These are more than just markings," Betty murmured. "These look like proper sentences." She shook her head and stepped back to take in the whole wall. "It's too much. My camera," she breathed, turning and striding to where she'd left her backpack. "I need my camera." She came back with her bag and pulled out a camera and handheld 3D scanner that looked like they could command the International Space Station.

"I'll leave you to it, then," Reg chuckled.

Suddenly, a low rumble vibrated beneath their feet; the shudder was enough to make Julia wonder if the sanctuary had just become aware of their intrusion.

"Something knows we're here," Dai-Lu said. "Let's just hope it isn't angry about it."

The sanctuary's walls nearest the entrance slowly started to glow. The mysterious light source grew in brilliance as it spread throughout the room, pushing away the darkness and revealing to them just how impossibly, unfathomably large the sanctuary was. The light revealed not only the scale, but architectural intricacies as well. The expanse was such that Julia could have easily believed it had been intended for a goddess. She walked, slowly, eyes wide, trying to take everything in.

"Remarkable," Dai-Lu murmured, moving away from the walls to the center of the room. She hadn't gone very far when she sucked in an audible breath.

"Oh, God."

Julia froze and called out to Dai-Lu. "What have you found?" she asked, hurrying to join her. But when Julia found what had commanded Dai-Lu's attention, she stopped so abruptly she almost tripped.

"What is it?" she asked.

At the core of the cavern, they found a colossal structure, resembling an egg lying on its side. It rested upon a massive, elevated pedestal that took up most of the room.

"That thing could take up an entire city block," Reg said.

As the room's illumination grew ever brighter, it became evident the egg in question was part of a larger, vastly intricate assembly. The colossal object sat regally upon its pedestal, cradled by a framework that defied both logic and gravity.

Encircling the egg was a ring, silver in color but crafted of a material that qualified neither as metallic nor ceramic. It was interwoven with a skeletal cylinder that suggested a single, unified design. Tubes constructed from the same silver mystery material spiraled around the ring. At regular intervals, these tubes intersected with thick, black cables emanating from the central cylinder, resembling the nervous system of an impossibly advanced organism.

As the cavern grew brighter, the light revealed dials and gauges, now inert and crusted with age. Control panels with smooth, glassy screens, some shattered, some intact, were integrated into the framework, suggesting they once displayed data streams or vital readouts. A series of symbols were etched near these screens, clearly intended for an operator familiar with their function. Circular access hatches were situated at various points on the ring.

Dai-Lu, a few steps ahead, felt an electrifying mix of familiarity and incredulity. "It resembles a torus reactor. But unlike any I've seen."

Sky sniffed the air curiously, circling the object.

"This must be their fusion reactor," Dai-Lu added after a few more moments. "Not like our tokamaks, but more advanced. A stellarator, maybe?" As she was the sole physicist in the room, it was clear she was talking to herself; no one else was qualified to engage in this level of dialogue with her. "Hmm. Maybe, maybe," she said, walking back and forth, taking in as many details as she could. "The tokamak reactors rely on external magnets and a toroidal—" here she remembered her audience and glanced over her shoulder. "That means 'doughnut-shaped.'"

"By all means," Julia said. "Go on."

"It relies, like I said, on a toroidal current to contain the plasma, while a stellarator solely uses external magnetic fields, which makes it more stable." She turned around to face the rest of the group, who were watching her in silence. "More stable but hellishly complex to design, mind you. Just look at the way these conduits are arranged. I think they're doing more than transporting energy; my guess is they're also meant to perform measuring and computing functions. A multi-purpose fusion reactor with embedded quantum calculations, perhaps?"

The team stood in awe, dwarfed by the imposing presence of the colossal reactor. Its intricate, alien geometry suggested a technology far surpassing anything they'd encountered so far. Dai-Lu was fixated on it, and Julia had no doubt her analytical mind whirring with possibilities and implications.

Suddenly Dai-Lu turned again, looking around. eyes searched the massive machine for any sign of the small tubes of metalized hydrogen they had come to find. "The key to this reactor is its fuel," she mumbled to herself. "Keep an eye out for any of those small tubes," she said to the others. "It's metalized hydrogen—that's the fuel it needs to run."

"Come, look at this!" James called out, his voice echoing off the walls. His flashlight cast a beam across something on the other side of the sanctuary.

Betty snapped a few more photographs before heading that way. Reg, Julia, Sky, and a reluctant Dai-Lu followed the sound of James's voice to see what he had discovered.

"Holy Mary, Mother of God," Reg said, his voice low and reverent.

The image set into the wall was at least fifteen feet tall. But its size wasn't its most unique aspect.

"That's the same depiction of the Eemians that Sam photographed inside the pyramid," Julia said. "And I think..." she stepped closer, looking at the female in the portrait. "And I think that's our Frigg."

"It's not the same," Reg said, moving closer and pointing to a corner of the portrait. "That's a different map."

"How can you tell?" Dai-Lu asked him.

Reg just shook his head. "Did I ask you how you knew impossible details about the giant Easter Egg over there? No, I did not."

Dai-Lu grinned and shrugged. "All right, that's a fair point."

As in the photograph Sam took in Antarctica, the portrait featured a tableau of nine humanoids standing in a pastoral setting. A family, perhaps. The adults wore white robes adorned with gold braid at the necklines and dark blue sashes at the waist. The adult male standing at the forefront of the image stood with his open palm extended, as if in offering. The woman at his side had luminous green eyes and long dark hair pulled back in a braid. At her ears she wore earrings with brilliant blue stones.

In the man's hand rested a gleaming black cylinder—the metalized hydrogen fuel sample Sam had recovered.

Even the children in the image were depicted the same way: they wore simpler versions of the adults' garments. Three were on the threshold of adolescence, while the others were younger, their faces and bodies soft with childhood.

Sky paced, walking from one end of the portrait to the other, unsettled. After several circuits, he lay down, resting his head on his paws, eyes intently on Julia. She crouched down and patted his side. "It's strange, I know. You're still a good boy, though."

"It's different, seeing it up close," Betty said softly. "They look . . . almost human. But something's different."

Dai-Lu nodded, coming to Julia's side. "It's the facial morphology—the proportions. Those eyes are disproportionately large compared to modern Homo sapiens norms. It's subtle, but it's there. Something adapted, evolved, or engineered."

"Our ancestors," murmured Betty.

Julia swept her flashlight across the rest of the space. The beam hit a reflective surface further back. "What's that?" she muttered to herself.

"What's what?" Reg asked, lifting his flashlight as well.

At that moment, the room's illumination function cascaded along this portion of the room, bathing everything in light. The reflective surface, whatever it was, glinted at Julia from behind a partition. Julia snapped off the flashlight and started walking towards yet another mystery, Betty and Reg close behind.

Behind the partition, Julia stopped cold, losing her breath.

"Oh, my God."

46

Green River Formation, Colorado

By the time Sam reached the mesa, a pillar of fire shot into the sky like some kind of biblical punishment. He couldn't begin to imagine the devastation if that flame broke its bounds, if a stray spark lit the sagebrush that would go up like so much tinder.

He slowed his vehicle, then stopped it entirely. People swarmed the area, fleeing the demonstration like panicked animals fleeing a forest fire. Though he was still about half a mile outside the main area, the crowds made further travel by car impossible.

The pillar of fire still burned. He couldn't begin to imagine how much gas was flaring off to keep it going. He pushed forward against the tide of protesters, dignitaries, and even folks with the words Empire Energy embroidered on their coveralls. A sheriff tried to get him to turn around, but Sam used the weight of his surname to keep moving toward the fire.

Soon, though the fire still burned, Sam found himself alone. The fences that had blocked the protestors were so much twisted metal, and he wasn't sure if it was because of the protestors trying to get in or his father's important visitors trying to escape. The heat battered him, more intense than anything he'd ever felt—except, perhaps, for the cold of Antarctica.

Just as he was giving up hope of making it further, the fire sputtered and died. Darkness fell so abruptly that it took Sam a good minute of blinking and disorientation to get anything resembling his night vision back. The heat died, too, and he began to regret leaving his coat in the car.

He stumbled through the dark toward the flare stack, calling his father's name, but when he arrived, the word froze on his tongue.

Magnus stood beside the crank, bent at the waist, hacking like a man who'd smoked two packs a day for sixty years, even though cigarettes had never been one of his vices. His suit coat was gone, and Sam could see through to Magnus's undershirt because the cotton shirt was sheer with sweat.

Tommy Jones lay at his father's feet, eyes open and staring right at Sam, a look of comingled triumph and horror frozen permanently on his features.

"What have you done?" Sam asked hoarsely, taking in his father's disheveled appearance. His proximity to Tommy. The haunted expression on his face.

"It's not what it looks like," Magnus said, lifting scorched and blistered hands. "Tommy, he went crazy. Completely lost it. Kept turnin' up the heat, kept—"

But Sam wasn't listening. He pushed his father aside and threw himself to his knees. Because behind Tommy's body lay John Grimes.

Sam's heart stuttered in his chest as if a hand had physically clenched around it. He reached for a pulse, fingers trembling, and the rush of relief when he found one brought a sob of gratefulness to his lips. "Have you called an ambulance?" he demanded.

Magnus blinked down at him, defensive platitudes still falling from his lips—*I know it looks bad; I know what it looks like; look, son, I had to stop him*—like so much bullshit.

"Magnus," Sam snapped. Not Dad. Maybe not Dad ever again. "Have you called an *ambulance*?"

But Magnus was either too shocked or too desperate to answer.

Sam fumbled for his phone. Now that the fire had died, the cold air licked at the sweat, chilling him deeply. When Sam started to explain the situation to the emergency services operator on the other end of the line, Magnus seemed to come back to himself. "I didn't have anything to do with this," he insisted. "Sam, I was trying to stop him from destroying everything. He was crazy. Batshit crazy. He wanted to burn the whole world down. It was like the end of the world! He's the one who—"

Sam acknowledged this interruption with a swift cutting motion.

"Son. Sam. You gotta believe me—you gotta—"

"*Shut up!*" Sam snarled. "For once in your fucking life, shut up! This is bigger than you. This is more *important* than you!"

Magnus stumbled back a step as though Sam's words had physically struck him. "Grimes," he whispered. "Oh, God. Oh, Lord. I didn't even see him there—I didn't even see—"

"Have you ever?" Sam said.

And finally, finally, Magnus fell silent.

The medical chopper arrived in record time. While the paramedics worked to stabilize Grimes for air travel, Sam grabbed Magnus's arm and pulled him to the side. The air still reeked of smoke and gas and chaos. In the distance, people shouted. Screamed. Magnus didn't protest the manhandling. He hadn't spoken a word since he realized what had happened to Grimes.

It was like the end of the world.

"Is he gonna make it?" Magnus asked without looking up from his feet.

"He's going to have the best medical care money can buy," said Sam. "Because I'll be footing the bill using the money you've been stealing from me."

This brought Magnus's head up fast, but before he could speak, Sam said, "Yeah. I found Grandpa Henry's will. I found out that the reason you've always been so damned insistent that I work at Empire isn't about me at all—it's about the money my grandfather set aside for me, with the caveat that I wouldn't have access to it unless I worked for the company."

"Son, I—it's your legacy—"

"How many times do I have to tell you? I. Don't. Care. I don't want to be part of a legacy of destroying the planet for profit. I want Empire to fall." Sam leaned close, forcing Magnus to meet his eyes. "I don't know what happened between you and Tommy Jones. I don't want to know. But I know that if I tell anyone what I saw, it won't look good for you. So, let's call this our mutually assured destruction. You keep me on Empire's books. You keep Grandpa Henry's inheritance flowing into *my* bank account instead of the one you 'set up' for me." Magnus tried to speak, but Sam raised his voice, silencing him again. "You let me go, you let John go, and you don't breathe a single word about either of us ever again—not to the press, not to the authorities. And if you ever say the word 'legacy' to me again, I'll go on record saying I saw you kill Tommy Jones with your bare hands."

"Sam, you're emotional. You're taking this out of context. I was looking out for you, son. I was—"

"There's only room for one more in the chopper," Sam said. "Find your own way back to hell. As of today, my father is as dead to me as your son has always been to you—except, of course, when you needed to use him. I'm done, Magnus. I'm done."

Magnus turned his head and spit on the ground. After a moment, the old mask that Sam knew so well settled over Magnus's features. "Empire Energy is about to become one of the most powerful companies in the world. And where will you be? Rotting in some underfunded university? Good riddance."

Sam smiled a slow smile. "No, Magnus. I'm going to help find the key to fusion energy, and I'm going to make your whole goddamn empire obsolete."

The paramedics called for Sam, then, and he turned away from Magnus and jogged toward the helicopter. Inside, he took Grimes's hand in his and gave it a comforting squeeze.

He didn't look back. Not once. Not even for a moment.

47

Kjerkfjorde Caves, Norway, January, 22

Built into the wall was a long series of stasis chambers, consisting of twenty or thirty individual pods, all filled with fluid. Most of them were occupied with women in varying stages of pregnancy.

Someone had painted a mural around the pods, featuring the goddess Frigg—or, if you preferred, the Eemian mother—kneeling in a meadow surrounded by other mothers and their children.

"What is this?" Reg asked. "What... *is* it?"

"It's... the shrine to Frigg," Julia replied. "Goddess of motherhood, children, and prophecy."

"Motherhood and children—that's easy enough to see. But where does the prophecy part fit in?" he asked.

"Think about the mural we saw on the way down here. Ragnarok. The end of the world. If they'd already gone through it once, they knew the world would likely go through it again. Maybe societies don't ever learn from their own mistakes. Maybe we're destined to make the same ones over and over again."

"And this is--"

"Nora!" Gale ran up to the stasis chamber, throwing himself against one of the pods, fists hammering the thick glass as he wept, sobbing her name over and over. Inside the pod was a woman who appeared much younger than Gale, and Julia wondered—not for the first time—how long he'd been living alone in a cave.

Lars came up behind Julia. "How long has this been going on?" he asked, his voice low.

"I couldn't begin to guess," Julia replied, walking closer to the stasis pods. Above each pod, a character was etched into the graphene. "Betty," Julia called out. "Do you have any idea what these markings indicate?"

Betty shone her flashlight, illuminating the characters, walking from one end of the chamber to the other, deep in thought.

"I recognize enough of them to know they're numbers," she said, finally. "They may be dates, but not dates as we understand them. It's something that has come up in Francois' translation program—their calendar was different than ours is now." She paced the length of the chamber again. "The best I can tell, these numbers are separated by a factor of twenty. That may be twenty years, it could be twenty months, it could be twenty of something else entirely."

Julia stared at the women in the pods. "If we assume it's twenty years, then this has been going on for well over a century."

"How do we get them out?" Reg asked.

"And *should* we?" Dai-Lu asked quietly, keeping one eye on Gale. "If this machinery is still working—and that appears to be the case," what else will we set off by letting them all out? Especially if they're all meant to be released later."

"We can't stay much longer. We need to gather what we can and get the hell out. So are you suggesting we should just leave them here?" Julia asked, arching an eyebrow at Dai-Lu.

"No," she said. "I'm saying I'll stay."

Julia stared at her. "Excuse me?"

"I'll stay," Dai-Lu said again. "I'm staying. I haven't even scratched the surface here. You can't expect me to be up to speed on this level of technology after, what, an hour? Even if I took photographs—do you think photographs will be enough? I don't."

"But--"

"Listen. I brought a sleeping bag, food, water, supplies—I can stay."

Betty walked away from the line of stasis pods to stand shoulder to shoulder with Dai-Lu. "She may have a point. We may never get another chance like this."

"Do you want to stay, too?" Julia shook her head. "That was never the plan."

Betty shrugged. "I'm only saying I wouldn't mind a few days to gather more writing samples. The more data I bring back, the more efficient Fran's translation program will be."

Julia stared at them both, dumbfounded. "Listen to yourselves. We don't know the first thing about the security of this place. Something here *kidnapped women* without so much as a blip on anyone's radar. Do we have any idea how that happened?"

"Give me time and I'll figure—"

"We are leaving and coming back with more resources. This is not up for debate," Julia said.

"That's admirably pragmatic of you," Dai-Lu countered. "But did it ever occur to you that this structure, the technology within, might actually provide what we need to survive?"

"I'm not willing to gamble your lives on that kind of guess," Julia shot back. "We don't know why these people disappeared, but if they're using Ragnarok in their imagery, I don't want to stick around only to be caught flat-footed."

"I'm not staying *forever.* Just a few days. I can't just walk away now. I need time to do the job Harry hired me to do, and I cannot figure out a reactor *like that* in an hour."

"Think about it—"

"I have."

"Have you? Have you *really?* We don't know a damn thing about this place. The sanctuary itself could be vulnerable to environmental changes. With the sanctuary door open, a rising tide could flood us out before we even knew what hit us."

Suddenly a warm hand rested on her shoulder. Julia whipped her head around, surprised. It was Gale, looking blotchy and tearstained, but more lucid than he had all day.

"I will stay with her. I've survived in these caves for years. She will not die." He offered an apologetic smile. "I will keep her safe. My Nora is here. She is *here.* I cannot lose her again."

"Julia," Dai-Lu said, "you're right about the risks, but great risk yields great rewards. This place—this sanctuary—is an anomaly, a cosmic hiccup in human history. I can't walk away from it now. Your responsibility to keep us safe is commendable, but part of that duty is also to not hold us back from a breakthrough. What if the next big leap for mankind is hidden within these walls? Are you willing to delay that discovery out of an overabundance of caution?"

Before Julia could respond, Sky leapt to his feet, lip curled in a low, menacing growl, hackles raised all down his back, his tail rigid and low. Julia turned to see what the dog was looking at, but she saw nothing. Slowly, she walked to Sky's side. "What is it, boy?" she asked, resting a hand on the dog's tense shoulders.

Then, in a blur of movement, Sky swung his head to the side, where James stood, his open backpack on the floor and a pistol in his hand, aimed at her head. Sky lowered his head, muzzle wrinkling, and let out a single, deep bark that filled the cavern and hurt Julia's ears.

"Control your dog, Julia," he said, offering a mocking little smile. "He's so vicious. I may get nervous and just . . ."

James turned and with astonishing accuracy, shot a bullet in Reginald' thigh. Reg fell to the ground, blood oozing from the wound as he clutched his leg, shouting in pain.

James shrugged. "Oops. I suppose I got nervous."

Gale stared at James, open mouthed. "*Draugr,*" he whispered. "He is *draugr.*"

"No, sorry. Nothing but plain old boring flesh and blood, you psychotic old coot."

Suddenly, Sky's growl grew in volume and intensity until he exploded in a torrent of snarling barks.

But he wasn't barking at James.

In the cavern's entrance stood a colossal figure, swathed in a ghastly hood crafted from the upper half of a lion's head, the feline ears pricked forward to resemble twisted horns. A row of yellowed teeth framed the hood, forming a grotesque halo over the wearer's deathly pale face.

The intruder pushed back the hood, revealing long black hair and terrifyingly brilliant green eyes set under thick brows. A dark beard came to a point at his chin, framing lips curled in a malevolent smile.

"Uzziel," Julia whispered, spitting out his name like a curse.

AFTERWORD

Read the exciting conclusion to Eemians in Book Three:

The Secret of Eschaton

By Paul McGowan

BOOKS IN THE EEMIAN SERIES

Book One

The Aurora Project

We were not the first

Book Two

Green Fires Burning

The World is About to Change

Book Three

The Secret of Eschaton

Endgame

Book Four

They Came First

In the Beginning

Made in United States
Orlando, FL
27 October 2024